Panda Books
Miss Sophie's Diary and Other Stories

DING Ling was born in 1904 in Linfeng, Hunan. In 1927, she published her first work "Meng Ke" which caught the attention of the literary world. In 1928, she produced her first story collection *In the Dark*.

In 1930 Ding Ling joined the progressive League of Left-wing Writers and became chief editor of its magazine *The Dipper*. From 1931 to 1933, she wrote many stories about the lives of workers and peasants. She was imprisoned by the Kuomintang government between 1933 and 1936. After her release, she became chief editor of the literary supplement to *Liberation Daily* and wrote "New Belief", "When I Was in Xia Village", "Night" and "Joining the Army".

From 1946 to 1948, Ding Ling completed her long novel *The Sun Shines over the Sanggan River*. A winner of the second Stalin Prize for Literature in 1951, it has now been translated into many languages.

Ding Ling is now deputy chairman of the Chinese Writers' Association and is currently writing her long novel *In the Coldest Days*.

Panda Books
First edition 1985
Copyright 1985 by CHINESE LITERATURE
ISBN 0-8351-1166-0

Published by CHINESE LITERATURE, Beijing (37), China
Distributed by China International Book Trading Corporation
(GUOJI SHUDIAN) P.O. Box 399, Beijing, China
Printed in the People's Republic of China

Miss Sophie's Diary and Other Stories

Ding Ling

Translated by W. J. F. Jenner

Panda Books

Contents

Foreword   7

Translator's Note   9

Miss Sophie's Diary   13

Shanghai in the Spring of 1930(2)   65

From Dusk to Dawn   122

The Hamlet   133

A Certain Night   180

Rushing   187

The Reunion   207

When I Was in Xia Village   236

Night   262

Foreword

WHEN the editors of *Chinese Literature* told me that this volume of my short stories had been translated into English by W.J.F. Jenner and was about to go to the printer they expressed the hope that I would write something as a foreword to it. The invitation was one I was happy to accept as I wanted this chance of saying a few words to readers of English.

About seventy years ago, when I was ten, I went on from reading many of the classical Chinese novels to my first contacts with the literature of Western Europe. At the time I knew little about European history or geography, and even less about European politics, economics or society, but I was soon lost in the world of Dickens. I wandered through the streets of London with his earls, marquises, aunts, boys and girls. I experienced something of the fogs and the April showers, and shared both the warm and the hard lives of the characters in his books. Later my range extended to France and Germany, and I visited nineteenth-century Russia too. After the May Fourth Movement of 1919, Western European culture and thought was spread very widely in China, and people of my generation were eager to "learn from the West". I can say that if I had not been influenced by Western literature I would probably not have been able to write fiction, or at any rate not the kind of fiction included in this collection. It is obvious that my earliest stories followed the path of Western realism, and not only in their forms: the thinking behind them was to some extent influenced by Western democracy. A little later, as the Chinese revolution developed, my fiction changed with the needs of the age and of the Chinese people. Its subject-matter, its characters and the life in them became Chinese. Yet in some pieces traces of European approaches can still be seen, especially in the stories from the 1920s and 1930s in this collection. That was why the translator of the French edition of these stories, Suzanne Bernard, said that the heroines of these stories, such as Sophie and Miss Tertia, would find friends abroad. I believe this may well be so. Literature ought to join minds together in this way, turning ignorance into mutual understanding. Time, place and institutions cannot separate it from the friends it wins. When I was most naive and living in the dark era of feudalism I was receptive to the literature of the rising bourgeoisie. And in 1957, a time of spiritual suffering for me, I found consolation in reading much Latin American and African literature. Now that my book is going to Europe and the rest of the world I hope that it will help to increase the understanding of China abroad and the friendship between peoples. This is why I wish to express my sincere thanks to the translator, Mr Jenner.

The eve of National Day, 1984

Translator's Note

THE nine stories in this selection of Ding Ling's shorter fiction are printed in the approximate order of their writing. The selection is the author's own.

The earliest story, only the second Ding Ling published, is "Miss Sophie's Diary", which was written where it is set — in Beijing — in the winter of 1927-8. Soon after it was published in February 1928, making its author famous for the boldness with which it dealt with a young woman's sexual feelings, Ding Ling moved to Shanghai, where she was to live till she was seized by the authorities in 1933 and held under a kind of house arrest in Nanjing for three years. While in Shanghai she became much more committed to revolutionary politics than she had been before. The enthusiasm of a convert is apparent in "Shanghai in the Spring of 1930", written in October of that year. (There is a companion piece to this story in which the woman turns to revolution.) A reminder of the price that had to be paid for commitment is to be seen in "A Certain Night", her attempt at imaginatively reconstructing the last moments of the short life of her husband Hu Yepin, who like the unnamed hero of the story was machine-gunned to death in jail with other Communists and Leftists in February 1931. "From Night to Dawn", a story that is clearly autobiographical — its central character is actually writing one of Ding Ling's own stories — is more realistic, showing her own struggle to keep going after the catastrophe by continuing to write without even the company of her baby to comfort her: the child, like Ding Ling and Hu Yepin's own, has been sent away to be looked after by his mother's family after his father's death.

It is against this background that the somewhat idyllic picture of a family of simple, honest and warm peasants in "The Hamlet", the story that the heroine of "From Night to Dawn" is writing, should be understood. The political excitement that Miss Tertia brings to the Tian Family Village in Ding Ling's native Hunan Province is the influence of the radical peasant movement that spread during the revolutionary years of 1926 and 1927. There is, however, no pastoral prettiness about the village life which the men in "Rushing" leave behind them in their desperate attempts to make their livings in Shanghai. This story, written in 1933, shows Shanghai having nothing to offer them either: those who succeed in walking the long way home to their village are the lucky ones.

"The Family Reunion" dates from 1936, the year in which Ding Ling's unofficial detention ended. It too shows rural life as hopeless, only this time the despair is that of a minor gentry family fallen on hard times.

Soon after this story was written Ding Ling made her way to northern Shaanxi, where the Communist Party was preparing to resist the coming Japanese invasion. After the war began in 1937 she threw herself into the work of making propaganda for resistance. By 1941, when she wrote the last two stories included here, she was writing about the peasants of North China with a subtlety and perception that showed how much she had learnt from four years of living among them. "When I Was in Xia Village" is a work that deliberately avoids oversimplifications. There is no hiding the harshness of village morality that condemns a teenage girl who was first raped by the Japanese army and then stayed with them on Communist orders so as to gather information. It is not a story that calls for a straightforward emotional response by its readers in the way that much of her Shanghai and earlier wartime writing had. The self-righteousness combined with prurient curiosity of some of the village women who had not been raped or captured is hardly part of the usual propaganda picture of the peasantry.

The collection closes with another of Ding Ling's rural pieces, "Night". The village cadre broods over the difficulties he faces in his political work and longs to be rid of his ageing wife who will never bear him another child to replace the two who are dead. The promise of life and warmth offered by the woman next door has to be turned down for the sake of the cause. This is a much more realistic picture of a revolution in action than the naïveté of "Shanghai in the Spring of 1930".

Readers interested in finding out more about Ding Ling's writings would do well to consult Yi-tsi Mei Feuerwerker's *Ding Ling's Fiction* (Cambridge, Mass., 1982). Ding Ling's novel *The Sun Shines over the Sanggan River*, translated by Yang Xianyi and Gladys Yang, is published by the Foreign Languages Press, Beijing.

The translations in this book have been saved from

many errors by the careful checking of Yu Fanqin and other translators of the quarterly *Chinese Literature*. Responsibility for those that remain is mine.

W.J.F. Jenner
Beijing-Leeds

Miss Sophie's Diary

24 December

IT'S blowing again today. The wind woke me up before daybreak, then the attendant came in to light the stove. I knew that I'd never get back to sleep again, and that my head would start spinning if I didn't get up. If I lie there wrapped up in my quilt I brood too much on all those weird notions. The doctor says it would be better if I had plenty of sleep and plenty of food, didn't read and didn't think. But that's impossible. I never get to sleep before 2 or 3 a.m. and I wake up before dawn. Windy days like this make you think of too many disturbing things. Besides, you can't go out when it's blowing hard and what can you do stuck in your room with no books to read? I can't just sit here by myself doing nothing and waiting for the time to go by. I spend all day enduring and putting up with things and waiting for the time to go by, wishing the winter would pass quicker. Once it's warmer my cough is bound to get better. Then I'll be able to go south or to university, whichever I want. But this winter's too long.

I warmed my third drink of milk when the sun started shining on the window-paper. Yesterday I heated milk up four times. But though I warm it up so often I don't always drink it. It's a kind of exercise to build up my spirits and ward off irritation on a windy day like this. To be sure, it uses up a little bit of time, but sometimes it makes me more irritated than ever. That's why I didn't do it at all for the whole of last week. But when I couldn't think of any other solution I had to do it again to while the time patiently away. It's as if I were very old.

When the paper comes I read through it systematically. I start with the big headline stories of national news then go on to the summaries of world events and the gossip about this city. I read everything, even the pages on education, party propaganda, economics, and the price of 96 government stocks. When I've read all that I go through the advertisements for schools, the legal notices about cases over the division of family property, and even the advertisements for 606 medicine, panaceas, beauty lotions, plays, films. . . . Only when I know them all do I languidly drop the paper. Of course, I do occasionally find a new ad, but they're only for some silk shop's fifth or sixth anniversary sale, or else death notices with apologies to those not personally informed.

When I've read the paper and can't think of anything else to do all that's left is to sit by the stove and get into a bad temper. I'm now used to getting upset day in and day out at the things that irritate me. Every day my head aches when I hear the voices of the other guests shouting for the staff along the corridor outside my window. Their voices are so coarse, loud, raucous and monotonous: "Hot kettle, waiter!" or "Water for washing, waiter." Anyone could imagine how horrible it sounds. Then there's always someone talking at the top of his voice on the telephone downstairs. But it's terrifyingly lonely when there are no sounds, especially inside these four whitewashed walls. Wherever you sit they blankly block your view. If you try to escape by lying on your bed you're crushed by the ceiling, which is whitewashed too. I can't find anything that isn't disgusting — that pockmarked waiter, the cooked food that tastes of cleaning rags, the dirt on the window frames that are never wiped clean, the mirror above the wash-stand. Look at it one way and your face is over a foot long; turn your head just a little bit to the side and it pulls it into such a twisted shape you give yourself a fright. It's all enough to put you in a filthy mood. Perhaps I'm the only person affected this way. I wish I could find something new to get miserable over and fed up with. But everything new, whether good or bad, is too far away from me.

Wei came after lunch. As soon as I heard the special urgency of his leather shoes from the other end of the corridor my heart felt as relieved as when you get your first breath after being stifled. But I couldn't show it. When he came in all I could do was to gaze at him in silence. He thought I was still in a bad mood, grasped both my hands, and kept saying, "Sister, sister" over and over again. As for me, I smiled of course. I knew why. I understood perfectly well what's hidden behind those bounding pupils that look not at but under my eyes, and what he doesn't want people to know about. It's been such a long time you've been in love with me, Wei. But has he won me? Of course, it's not my fault at all. That's how a woman is supposed to behave. In fact I've been very straight with him. I don't believe that there's another woman who wouldn't have made a fool of him. Besides, I'm really and truly sorry for him. Sometimes I can't stop myself wanting to say to him, "Can't you change your tactics, Wei? The way you're acting only gets me down." Yes, if Wei weren't so stupid I could like him a lot better. But all he can do is to make this sincere parade of his devotion.

Wei was satisfied to see me smile. He sprang round the end of the bed to take off his overcoat and his big fur hat. If he'd looked back at me he'd surely have seen the misery in my eyes. Why doesn't he understand me a little better?

I've always wanted a man who could understand me completely. If he doesn't understand me, what's the use of his love and consideration? But my father, my older sister and my friends can only care for me in that blind way. I really don't know what it is about me that they care for. My arrogance? My temper? My T.B.? Sometimes I get angry and upset about it, but they only make even more allowances and are fonder of me than ever. The things they say to try to cheer me up are so wrong that they make me want to hit them even more than ever. At times like that I really long for somebody who'd understand me. Even if he insulted me I'd be happy and proud.

When nobody pays any attention to me or comes to see me I miss people or get angry with them. But when people do come to see me I can't help giving them a hard time. There's nothing I can do about that either. Recently I've tried to train myself and stop myself saying the things that come to my tongue in case I touch someone's hidden sensitive spots when I'm only joking. That's why the state of mind in which I was sitting with Wei can be imagined. But when Wei stood up and said he was going I began feeling miserable at the prospect of being lonely and started to hate him. This at least Wei has long understood, which is why he never goes before ten at night. But I'm not trying to deceive him or myself. I'm quite sure that, so far from doing him any good, staying late only makes me feel even more strongly than ever that he's too easy to push around, or be even sorrier for his incompetence in love.

28 December

Today I invited Yufang and Yunlin to the cinema. Yufang asked Jianru along. I was so angry I wanted to weep, but I laughed aloud. Jianru really does hurt my self-respect. In her looks and movements she's just like a friend I had when I was young, so I often found myself chasing her before I realized what I was doing. And she deliberately gave me a lot of the courage I needed to get close to her. Since then I've been treated intolerably and hated my shameless behaviour in the past whenever I've thought of it, but regrets can change nothing now. Once I sent her eight long letters in a single week, but she ignored them completely. Goodness only knows what Yufang thought she was up to, asking her here on purpose although she knew I didn't want the past brought up again. It's as if she deliberately wanted to make me angry. I was furious.

Yufang and Yunlin can't have noticed anything different about my smile. Jianru must have been able to. But she can put on an act, play stupid, and talk to me as if there were no quarrel between us. I was going to give her a piece of my mind, but just when the words were on the tip of my tongue I remembered the ban I'd imposed on myself. Besides, if I'd really told her what I thought she'd only have been more pleased with herself than ever. That's why I controlled myself and went out with them.

We got to the Zhenguang Cinema early and met a whole crowd of girls from home at the entrance. I'm sick of all those routine dimpled smiles so I cut them. For no good reason at all my bad temper extended to all the other people there to see the film. While Yufang was deep in a lively conversation with them I abandoned my guests and slipped back here.

I'm the only person who can forgive me. Everyone is criticising me, and none of them realize the impact that some people have on me when I'm with them. People say that I'm odd. Little do they realise how I'm constantly trying to make people like me and win their affection. But they don't give me enough encouragement to say things that run contrary to my heart. They're always giving me occasion to reflect on my own actions and be further estranged from them than ever.

It's very late now, and the whole hostel is quiet. I've been lying on my bed for a very long time. I've thought some things through very clearly. What have I got to be upset about?

29 December

Yufang phoned early this morning. She's a good person and could never lie, so I suppose Jianru really must be ill. Yufang said she'd got ill because of me, and wanted me to go over so that Jianru can explain some things to me. Yufang is wrong and Jianru is too. I'm not the sort of person who likes hearing explanations. I fundamentally deny the need for explanations in the universe. If friends get on well that's fine. And if you give people something of a bad time when you don't get on that's perfectly proper and respectable. I think I'm very generous and not nearly good enough at getting my revenge. If Jianru is ill on my account I'm delighted. I'm not going to refuse to believe the news that someone else is ill because of me. Besides, if Jianru is ill I won't feel quite as angry with myself as I have been.

I really don't know how to analyse myself. Sometimes I can be filled with a vague and indefinable misery when a cloud is broken up by the wind, but the sight of a man in his twenties (Wei is in fact four years older than me) shedding his tears drop by drop on the back of my hand makes me laugh with pleasure like a savage. Wei had come to see me with a lot of writing paper and envelopes he'd bought in the east city. As he was so happy and full of smiles I deliberately teased him and cheered up the moment I saw him crying. "Save your tears," I said, "and don't think I'm weak like other women who can't resist a tear. If you want to cry, go back home to cry. Tears get me down." Of course, he didn't go, defend himself or get angry. He just curled up at the edge of the chair and wept silently and openly. Goodness only knows where all those tears came from. I naturally started feeling ashamed of myself at being so delighted, so I told him like a big sister to wash his face and stroked his hair. He started smiling with tears still in his eyes.

When I was with this open and honest man I tortured him with all the cruelty of my nature. But when he'd gone I wanted to drag him back and make this little plea: "I know I was wrong. Please stop loving a woman like me who doesn't deserve your sincere devotion."

1 January

I don't know how people who like noise and bustle celebrated the New Year. All I did was to add an egg to my milk. The egg was one of the twenty Wei brought over yesterday. I boiled seven of them yesterday as tea-eggs. The thirteen that are left will probably last me a fortnight. I thought that if Wei came to lunch, there'd definitely be a chance of a couple of tins. I hoped he would come. As I wanted him to come I went to Xidan to buy four boxes of sweets, two packets of savouries and a basket of mandarin oranges and apples to give him when he came. I was certain that he'd be the only person to come today.

But I ate my lunch and Wei didn't come.

I wrote five letters altogether on the good paper and with the good brushes Wei bought for me a few days ago. I'd been hoping to receive some nice cards, but I didn't get any. Even my older sisters, who really enjoy that sort of thing, forgot that one thing they should have sent me. I don't mind about not having the cards, but I was upset that they forgot me. Too bad. It serves me right. I've never ever paid a New Year call on anyone.

I ate my evening meal alone too. I was thoroughly fed up.

This evening Yufang and Yunlin came, and they

brought a tall young man with them. I reckon that those two are really happy. Yufang has Yunlin to love her; she's satisfied and so is he. Happiness lies not so much in having a lover as in that the two of them have no greater wish. Quiet lives in which they can talk things over. Of course, some people would despise this sort of ordinariness. But that only applies to other people like that, not to my Yufang.

Yufang is a good person. Because she has Yunlin she wants "all the lovers in the world to be united". Last year she tried to arrange a love marriage for Mary, and she wants me and Wei to hit it off. That's why she asked me about him the moment she came. But she, Yunlin and that tall man ate all the things I'd bought for Wei.

The tall man's a real good looker. It's the first time I've ever been aware of male beauty: it's not something I'd ever noticed before. I always thought that there was nothing more to being a man than being able to talk, read people's expressions and be careful. Now I've seen this tall man I realise that men can be cast in another and a noble mould. He made Yunlin look so petty and stupid by comparison. I really feel sorry for Yunlin. He'd be so distressed at the coarseness of his expressions and behaviour if he knew how wretched he looked beside the tall man. Goodness knows what Yufang must feel when she compares the two men, the tall one and the short one.

How can I describe the beauty of that stranger? Of course, his tall body, his delicate white face, his thin lips and his soft hair would all dazzle anyone, but there's also an elegance about him that I can't express in words or put my hands on, but sets my heart aflame.

For example, when I asked him his name he handed me his card in an incredibly relaxed way. I looked up and saw the corners of his soft, red, and deeply inset mouth. Could I tell anyone how I looked at those two delightful lips like a child longing for sweets? But I know that in this society I'll never be allowed to take what I want to satisfy my impulses and my desires, even though it would do nobody else any harm. That's why I had to control myself, keep my head down, and silently read the name on the card: Ling Jishi from Singapore.

Ling Jishi could talk here without any constraints as if in a very old friend's place. I couldn't possibly say that he deliberately came to make a fool of a timid soul like me. I had to force myself to resist his attraction, so I never let myself raise my eyes to look at that lovely corner by the stove. It was so bad that my worn-out slippers, which I'd never felt embarrassed about before, wouldn't let me go into the lamplight by the table. I was angry with myself: why was I so awkward and humourless with him? Usually I despise the way other people pay attention to their social skills but today I know I seemed silly and stupid. Oh dear! He must have thought I was a girl straight up from the country.

Seeing how lifeless I looked Yunlin and Yufang thought that I'd taken against this stranger, so they kept interrupting him and took him away before long. Can I be grateful to them for their kind intentions? Watching the two short figures and one tall one disappearing in the yard downstairs I didn't want to go back into my room. It was still full of his footsteps, his voice, and the crumbs of the biscuits he'd been eating.

3 January

Last night and the night before I coughed all night. I
don't have any confidence in medicine. Medicine and
disease have nothing to do with each other: isn't that
so? I know perfectly well that I'm completely fed up
with that bitter potion, but I keep on taking my doses
on time. If I didn't take my medicine what other
hope would I have of a cure? God wants people to
live patiently, so he arranges so much suffering before
death that people want to keep their distance from it.
As for me, I seek the good things of life all the more
keenly because my life is going to be so rushed and
short. It's not because I'm afraid of death but because
I always feel that I've yet to enjoy everything life has
to offer. I want, I want to make myself happy. Day
and night I'm always dreaming of things that would en-
able me to have no regrets when I die. I imagine myself lying on a bed in an extremely luxurious bedroom,
my sisters kneeling on a bearskin rug beside the bed
praying for me, my father sighing quietly at the open
window, while I read lots of long letters that the people
who love me have sent me, and my friends weep sin-
cerely as they remember me. . . . I desperately need
these human emotions and want to possess all sorts of
impossible things. But what do people give me? For
two whole days I've been alone here as a prisoner in
this hostel with no visitors and no letters. I've lain on
my bed coughing, sat by the stove coughing, been to the
table coughing, and thought of those hateful people. . . . Actually, I have had a letter, but it only
added to my unhappiness. It was sent to me by a
strong coarse man from Anhui who pestered me a year

ago. I tore it up before I'd even finished it. All that "love, love" in it made my flesh creep. I despise the adoration of people I don't like.

But can I tell what I really need?

4 January

Things have gone very badly wrong. Why did I want to move, and why was I stupid enough to trick Yunlin as if lying were so instinctive to me that it came to me today without any trouble at all? If Yunlin realized that Sophie could trick him goodness knows how upset he'd be. They all love Sophie as if she were their little sister. Of course, I was uneasy about it and now I regret it. But can I make my mind up whether to move or not?

I have to tell myself, "You're longing for that tall man." Yes, for the last few days and nights there's been no time when I haven't been yearning for those things that allure me. Why hasn't he come alone to see me these last few days? He ought to realize that it's wrong of him to make me long for him like this. He ought to come to see me and tell me that he's been missing me too. If he came I wouldn't refuse to listen to him declaring his love for me. I'd let him know what I want. But he won't come. I suppose it's the sort of thing that happens in romances but not in real life. Surely I shouldn't have to go to see him. If a woman's as reckless as that she's bound to come to a bad end. Besides, I still need people's respect. I couldn't think of what to do, so I just had to go to Yunlin's first on the offchance. After lunch I braved the wind and went to the eastern part of town.

Yunlin is a student at the Metropolitan University

and he's rented a room in Youth Alley that's in between the university's first and second campuses. When I got there I was in luck: he hadn't gone out and Yufang hadn't yet arrived. Yunlin was of course surprised that I'd come out on so windy a day. I told him I'd dropped in on my way to a consultation at the German Hospital. He wasn't at all suspicious and asked about my illness. I deliberately led the conversation round to the other evening. I found out without any difficulty that the man lives in No. 4 Dormitory next to the university's second campus. Soon after that I started sighing and using every kind of language to describe the loneliness and boredom of life in my hostel in the western city. I lied and said that all I wanted to do was to be close to Yufang. (I knew that Yufang was already preparing to move to where Yunlin was living.) I asked Yunlin to take me to find a room nearby. Yunlin was of course delighted to do this job: he didn't hesitate.

We ran into Ling Jishi while we were looking for a room and he came along with us. I was very pleased, so pleased that I got bold enough to take several good hard looks at him. He didn't notice. When he asked about my illness I told him I was completely better. His smile suggested that he didn't believe me.

I liked the look of a tiny, low, mildewed eastern room in the Dayuan Hostel next door to Yunlin's. He and Yunlin both said it was too damp, but I insisted on moving in tomorrow because I was too fed up with the other place and desperately wanted to be close to Yufang. Yunlin had no choice but to agree, and he also said that he and Yufang would come to help me move first thing tomorrow.

Could I tell anyone the only reason why I chose that

room? It's because it's between No. 4 Dormitory and Yunlin's place.

He didn't say goodbye to me, so I went back to Yunlin's, talking and laughing with all the courage I could muster. I examined him in every detail. I felt the need to kiss him everywhere. Didn't he notice that I was sizing him up and working things out about him? Later I deliberately said that I wanted to ask him to give me some extra English lessons. Yunlin smiled, but he looked disconcerted and gave a vague embarrassed answer. I told my heart that he couldn't be a bad lot. Fancy a big man like him blushing. This made my fire burn more fiercely than ever. But I didn't want him to understand me and see me as a push-over, so I forced myself to leave and came back very early.

Thinking it all over carefully now I'm worried that my impetuosity may have got me into an even worse mess. For the time being I'd better remain in this room heated by an iron stove. Do I have to admit that I've fallen in love with that overseas Chinese? I know nothing about him at all. His mouth, his brows, his eyes, his fingertips . . . all mean nothing. They aren't what one ought to need. If that's what I think about I've been bewitched. I've made my mind up not to move, but to concentrate all my efforts on recovering my health.

I've decided. I regret now the wrong things I did today, all the things a lady should never do.

6 January

It's all my fault. When they heard I'd moved Jin Ying came from the south city and Jiang and Zhou from the west city to my damp, low-ceilinged little room. I laughed and was even rolling about on the bed at times, so that both of them said I was getting more and more childish. That made me laugh aloud and long to tell them what I was thinking of. Wei too came this afternoon. He was very upset that I'd moved: I hadn't discussed it with him and it was taking me further away from him. When he saw Yunlin he ignored him completely. Not understanding why Wei was in such a bad temper, Yunlin stared at him, only for Wei to look grimmer than ever. I wanted to laugh, but I said to myself, "Poor thing, you've treated him very unfairly. He's a good man."

Yufang has stopped talking about Jianru to me. She's decided to move to Yunlin's place in the next two or three days. As she feels I'm so keen to be near her she won't let me stay here all alone. She and Yunlin are showing me even more warmth than ever.

10 January

I've seen Ling Jishi on each of the last few days, but we've said very little to each other. I'm certainly not going to be the first to bring up the extra English lessons. It makes me laugh to see him going to visit Yunlin twice a day. I'm sure he was never as close to Yunlin before. I haven't invited him to my place once, even though he's asked me several times how the move has gone. The only answer I give is a smile as if I didn't understand what he's getting at. I'm giving all my mind to this. It's as if I were involved in a struggle with something, something I want but won't go after.

I must find a way of making him give it himself. Yes, I understand myself, I'm only a completely female woman. Women devote all their thoughts to the men they want to conquer. I want to possess him. I want him to give his heart unconditionally and kneel before me, begging me to kiss him. I've gone completely mad. I just keep thinking over and over again of the tricks and methods I'm going to use. I've gone right off my head.

Yufang and Yunlin didn't notice how excited I was getting. They just said that I'd soon be better. I didn't want them to understand, so when they said I was getting better I pretended to be pleased.

12 January

Yufang has moved in, but Yunlin has moved out. Can there be another couple like them in the universe? They won't live together for fear of having a child. I imagine that they can't be certain that if they lay in each other's arms in bed they wouldn't do other things too, which is why they're taking this precaution against that sort of physical contact. Hugging and kissing when they're alone isn't dangerous, so the occasional discreet bout doesn't come within the scope of their ban. I couldn't help laughing at them for their asceticism. Why shouldn't you embrace the naked body of your beloved? Why repress that manifestation of love? How can the pair of them think of those irrelevant and worrying things before they're even under the same quilt? I don't believe that love can be so rational and scientific.

They didn't get angry with me for teasing them.

They're proud of their purity, and they laughed at my childishness. I can understand their state of mind, but there are so many strange things in the world that I can't fathom at all.

I stayed at Yunlin's (or Yufang's, as I should now say) till 10 before coming back. We talked a lot about ghosts.

I got used to talk about ghosts when I was tiny. I often used to sit on my aunt's lap listening to my uncle telling stories from *Liaozhai,* and I loved listening till late at night. As for being frightened, that was another matter. I'd never tell anyone about it, because if I'd admitted being frightened I'd never have heard the story to the end, my uncle would have gone into his study, and I'd not have been allowed to get out of bed. When I went to school I learnt a little science from the teachers. Because I was completely convinced by our teacher Pockmarked Zhou I believed the books too, whereupon ghosts weren't frightening any more. Now I'm more grown up I still say that I don't believe in ghosts, but my disbelief doesn't stop the goose-pimples or my hair standing on end. But whenever the conversation gets on to ghosts other people don't realize that I'm wanting to change the subject because I'm afraid of lying alone in my quilt at night being sad at missing my dead aunt and uncle.

When I came back and saw that dark alley I did feel a little scared. I wouldn't have been at all surprised if a great yellow face had appeared in some corner or if a hairy hand had stretched out in that alley that seem-ed to be frozen solid. But that tall man Ling Jishi seemed a reliable bodyguard to have beside me, so when Yufang asked me I said I wasn't scared.

Yunlin came out with us and went back to his new place. As he went south and we went north the sound of his rubber-soled shoes on the footpath died out within three or four paces.

He put out a hand and took me by the waist.

"I'm sure you're frightened, Sophie."

I tried to struggle but I couldn't break free.

My head rested against his ribs. I wondered what sort of creature I'd look like in the light, held in the arms of a man over a head taller than me.

I ducked down and got out. He let go and stood beside me as we knocked at the front gate.

The alley was very dark, but I could see very clearly where he was looking. My heart was pounding somewhat as I waited for the gate to open.

"You're frightened, Sophie," he said.

There was the sound of the bolts being drawn as the porter asked who was there. I turned to him and started to say, "Goodnight." He seized my hand fiercely and I couldn't finish the word. The porter showed his astonishment as he saw the tall man behind me.

When the two of us were alone in the room my boldness was not needed any longer. I deliberately tried to make some politely conventional remarks but just couldn't. All I could manage was, "Do sit down." Then I began washing my face.

Goodness knows how, but I'd forgotten all about ghosts.

"Are you still interested in studying English, Sophie?" he asked suddenly.

So he was coming to me, and he was the first to bring up the English. Of course he wouldn't necessarily be pleased at having to sacrifice his time for nothing to give some extra classes: he couldn't fool me, a woman of twenty, about what he had in mind. I smiled, though only in my head.

"I'm too stupid," I said. "I'm worried that I couldn't manage it and would only make a fool of myself."

He said nothing, but picked up a photograph that was standing on my table. It was of my sister's little girl. She's just one year old.

When I'd washed my face I sat down at the other side of the table. He looked first at me, then at the little girl, then back at me again. Yes, she looked very much like me.

"She's nice, isn't she?" I asked him. "Do you think she's like me?"

"Who is she?" His voice clearly showed that he was very serious.

"Don't you think she's sweet?"

He kept asking me who she was.

Suddenly I realized what he was driving at. I wanted to lie to him.

"She's mine." I snatched the photograph and kissed it.

He believed me. I'd actually fooled him. I felt triumphant in my dishonesty.

This triumph seemed to make him less charming and handsome. Why else could I have ignored his eyes and forgotten his mouth when he showed that naive astonishment? Otherwise this triumph was bound to cool my passion.

But after he'd gone I felt sorry. There'd been so many obvious chances set in front of me. If only I'd made some other expression when he pressed my hand and let him understand that I wouldn't have turned him down he'd certainly have made some bolder moves. When it comes to boldness between the sexes I'm absolutely certain that as long as you don't detest the other person the pleasure you feel must be like the body melting. So why do I have to be so prim and proper with him? After all, what did I move into this dilapidated room for?

15 January

I'm not lonely now. During the day I'm next door, and in the evenings I've got another new friend to talk to. But my illness is getting worse. It really gets me down: whatever I want is useless to me. Am I hankering after something? Everything is so ridiculous, but to my surprise the thought of death makes me feel even more miserable. Whenever I see Dr. Klee's expression I think: Yes, I understand, say what you like, there's no hope for me now. But I put on a smile instead of weeping. Nobody knows how many tears I shed in the middle of the night.

Ling Jishi has come for several evenings running. He tells people he comes to help me with my English, but when Yunlin asked me about it all I could do was to say nothing. This evening I put my copy of *Poor People* in front of him and he really did start teaching me. Then I had to push the book aside and say, "Don't tell people any more that you're helping me with my English. I'm ill, so nobody will believe you." "Sophie," he was quick to reply, "couldn't I teach you when you're a bit better? As long as you'd like me to, Sophie."

This new friend might seem to be a very desirable

person, but for some reason I don't understand I can't be bothered with any of that sort of thing. When I watch him leave every evening, having got no joy at all, I feel rather guilty and awkward. As he was putting his overcoat on I had to say to him, "Forgive me. I'm ill." He misunderstood me and thought I was just making a polite remark. "That doesn't matter at all. I'm not afraid of catching it." Later I thought it over carefully. Perhaps he was referring to something else. I can't be sure that other people's actions are as simple as I imagine.

16 January

Today I had a letter from Yun in Shanghai that has plunged me even deeper into despair. I could find no words with which to comfort her. "My life and my love are useless to me now," she wrote. So she has less need than ever for consolation from me and the tears I shed for her. I can guess from her letter what her life has been like since her marriage, even though she won't tell me in as many words. Why does God have to play such cruel tricks on people in love? Yun is highly strung and very passionate. Of course she wouldn't be able to stand that gradual cooling, or a lack of feeling that can no longer be concealed. I wish she'd come to Beijing, but is it possible? I doubt it.

When Wei came I showed him Yun's letter. He was really upset by it because the man who makes her feel that her life is pointless is, alas, his own elder brother. So I told him a lot about my new "philosophy of life", and he did the only thing that instinctively he can: he cried. I could only watch very coldly as his eyes turned red and he wiped them with his hands, and I gave him every kind of cruel explanation of what he was doing. I never imagined that he could be an exception, an honest person in the world. Before long I slipped out.

Because I wanted to avoid everyone I knew I stayed by myself in the cold, lonely park till very late. I don't know how I got through all that time. All I could think was, "It's so meaningless. The sooner I die the better."

17 January

I think I may be going off my head. I'd be very happy to do so if I really could. I reckon that if I went mad I wouldn't be aware of life's troubles any longer.

Today I started drinking hard after keeping off it for six months because of my illness. I could see quite clearly that what I spewed up was blood even redder than the wine. But I felt as though something else was in charge of my heart. It was as if the drink was going to kill me tonight and I didn't want to go on thinking about all those tiresome complications.

18 January

I'm still in this bed. Soon I'm going to leave this room, perhaps for ever. Can I be certain that I'll have the happiness of touching these pillows and quilt of mine again? Yufang, Yunlin, Wei, Jin and Xia were all sitting around me in silence, anxiously waiting for the dawn so that they could take me into hospital. It was the sound of their gloomy mutterings that woke me up. I didn't want to speak; I was thinking about what had happened yesterday morning. The smell of the drink and vomit left in the room made me notice that my heart was in acute pain; the tears flowed again. Their silence, like the desolation and gloom on their faces, seemed like signs that my death was imminent. If I were to go to sleep for ever in this way would they sit around my stiff corpse in silence like that? When they saw I'd woken up they came around me and asked how I was. That was when I felt the full horror of death and separation. I held their hands and gazed closely into each of their faces as if I wanted to remember this for ever. Their tears fell on my hands as if they realised that I was going to leave them finally for the land of death. Wei especially was crying so much he made himself look terrible. Oh dear, I thought, cheer me up a bit, friends. That made me smile. I asked them to sort some things out for me, and they pulled the big rattan case out from under the bed. Inside it there were some bundles wrapped up in embroidered handkerchiefs. "I want those to take into the Union Hospital," I said. When they passed the bundles to me I showed them that they were all full of letters. "Look," I said to them with a smile, "yours are here too." That seemed to cheer them up a bit. Wei quickly handed me a photograph album from the drawer as if he wanted me to take that too. That made me smile even more. There were seven or eight pictures of him in it, and as a special concession I let him kiss my hand and rub it against his face, which stopped the room feeling as though there were a corpse lying in it. Just then the sky began to show the greyish white of dawn and they all began to get busy, rushing around to find me a rickshaw. And thus my hospital life began.

4 March

It's twenty days since I had the cable about Yun's death, but my health has been improving daily: On the 1st the people who'd brought me into hospital took me back to the hostel, where my room had been beautifully tidied up. Because they were worried I'd feel the cold they'd lit a little iron coal stove for me. I didn't know how to thank them, especially Wei and Yufang. Jin and Zhou stayed with me for a couple of days before going. They were my nurses and I could lie in bed all day. I was so comfortable it was just like being at home, not at all like being in a hostel. Yufang has decided to stay with me for a few more days. When it's warmer she'll find me a place to convalesce in the Western Hills. I'd love to get out of Beijing, but although it's March it's still so cold. As Yufang insists on staying I won't refuse, so the little bed that was put up a few days ago for Jin and Zhou won't be taken down.

Being in the hospital was also good for my heart: it really and truly was warmed up again by the kindness those friends showed me, and I feel once more that the universe is full of love. Especially Ling Jishi. When he came to see me in the hospital I felt very proud. I thought that only someone as handsome as him was fit to visit a woman friend in hospital. I was also aware that the nurses were all jealous of me. One day that very beautiful Miss Yang asked me, "What's that tall man to you?"

"A friend." I disregarded the rudeness of her question.

"From your province?"

"No. He's an overseas Chinese from Southeast Asia."

"Then is he a fellow-student of yours?"

"No."

Whereupon she gave a knowing smile.   "Then he's just a friend?"

Of course, I didn't have to blush, and I could have said a few words to warn her off the subject, but I was embarrassed. Only when she saw the embarrassed way in which I shut my eyes and pretended I was going to sleep did she go away, wearing a self-satisfied grin. From then onwards I was always in a bad mood with her. To avoid trouble I lied that Wei was my brother whenever people asked me about him. There was one boy who is very close to Zhou. I pretended that he came from my province or was a relation.

When I was alone in the room after Yufang had gone to her classes I looked through all the letters I'd received in the last month or more. I was both pleased and satisfied that so many people had remembered me. I need people to remember me: the more people who feel friendly towards you the better.   As for my father, that goes without saying. He sent me another photograph, but it looks as though he's got a few more white hairs. My older sisters are both well, but their children keep them too busy to be able to write to me often.

Ling Jishi came back before I'd finished reading the letters. I tried to stand up, but he held me down. When he squeezed my hand I could have wept for joy.

"Did you think I'd ever come back to this room?" I asked him.

He glanced at the spare bed at the side of the room with visible disappointment. I told him that the two women who'd been staying with me had gone and that this was kept there for Yufang.

When he heard this he told me that he hadn't wanted to come back today in case Yufang would get fed up with him. That made me feel happier than ever.

"Aren't you worried that I'll get fed up with you?" I said.

He sat at the head of the bed, telling me even more about how he'd been living this last month or more — his clashes with Yunlin and their arguments because he had thought that I should come out of hospital earlier but Yunlin had insisted that I couldn't. Yufang had sided with Yunlin. Ling Jishi had realised that as he hadn't known me for very long his opinions wouldn't carry any weight so he dropped the matter and had left earlier whenever he met Yunlin at the hospital.

I knew what he was driving at, but I pretended not to and said, "You're running Yunlin down, but I'd never have got out of the hospital without him. I was much more comfortable there."

I saw him silently tilting his head to one side. He didn't reply.

He reckoned that Yufang would soon be back, so he went, quietly saying he'd be back tomorrow. Yufang did indeed come back soon after. She didn't ask and I didn't tell her. As I'm ill she didn't want to waste my energy by making me talk too much. I was glad to use this as an excuse to think about other, trivial things.

6 March

When Yufang went to her lectures, leaving me alone in the room, I started thinking about the peculiar things that happen between men and women. In fact, without wishing to boast, I've had more, even several times more, training than my friends have. But recently I haven't been able to understand it all. When I'm alone with that tall man my heart starts pounding and I feel ashamed and frightened, while he just sits there casually talking about his past with something like naivety, squeezing my hand from time to time. He does it ever so naturally, but my hand can't rest calmly in his big one and it gradually gets hot. The moment he stood up to go I couldn't help getting desperate and feeling that I was about to fall into a terrifying panic.

I stared at him, but I don't know whether it was a plea for pity or a look of resentment. He ignored my look. Even if he did happen to understand it all he said was, "Yufang's coming." What could I have said? He's afraid of Yufang! Of course, I wouldn't want anyone to know about the shocking things I think about in secret by myself, though recently I've also felt that I need people to understand my emotions. I've tried to talk about my feeling in a roundabout way with Yufang, but she just faithfully puts my quilt over me and worries about my medicine. Really, I can't help being a bit irritated.

8 March

Yufang has moved out now, but Wei wants to replace her as nurse. I know that Wei would be much better than Yufang. If I wanted some tea in the night I wouldn't have to bury my head in my bedclothes and forget about it because I could hear her snoring away and didn't want to disturb her. Of course I turned down his kind offer, but he insisted. I had to say, "It'd be very awkward for me if you were here. Besides, I'm not ill now." Then he pointed out that the room next door was empty and he could stay there. I was at my wits' end when Ling Jishi came. I thought they didn't know each other, but Ling Jishi grasped Wei's hand and said they'd met a couple of times at the hospital. Wei was very cold and ignored him. "This is my younger brother," I said to Ling Jishi with a smile. "He's only a boy and doesn't know how to behave in public. You must come more often and get to know him." Wei really did turn into a miserable-looking little boy who stood up and went. I felt very upset because there was someone else present, but I had to hide it. I felt a little guilty towards Ling Jishi, but he wasn't at all bothered. Instead he asked me, "But isn't his surname Bai? How did he turn into your brother?" I laughed. "Do you only let the Lings call you brother?" He laughed too.

These days young people like talking about "love" whenever they're together. Even though I may know a little about it I can't really explain it when it comes down to it. I think I know perfectly well about those little movements that men and women make together. Perhaps it's just because I know about those movements that I'm so confused about "love", that I don't have the courage to advocate love, that I can't believe in myself as a pure and lovable girl, and that I'm suspicious of what the world calls "love" and of the love I've received.

When I was just beginning to understand something of life those who loved me gave me a very hard time by giving a lot of people who were not involved the chance to despise and humiliate me. In the end my dearest friends abandoned me. Later I was so intimidated by love that I had to leave my school. Although I grow up a little every day, I've always been aware of all those pointless complications, which is why I'm sometimes suspicious of "love" and even despise that kind of intimacy. Wei says he loves me, but why does he keep making me miserable? This evening, for example, he came here again and cried, and with great intensity at that. It made no difference when I said, "Tell me, what's the matter?" and, "Talk, Wei, I beg you." He just ignored me. This is something that has never happened before. I tried as hard as I could, but I couldn't guess what catastrophe had hit him. I didn't know what to guess. Later on he must have had enough crying because he shouted, "I hate him." "Who's been bullying you?" I asked. "Why all the shouting and yelling?" "I hate that tall man. The one you're so thick with." That's when I realised that he was in a sulk with me. I couldn't help smiling. Is this tiresome jealousy, this selfish possessiveness, love? I smiled, and my smiles were of course no consolation for that man and his wild ambitions. My contempt made him lose all control of his temper. At the sight of his blazing eyes I imagined he was going to bite and thought, "Come here!" But he just bowed his head, started crying again, and lurched out, wiping his eyes.

This performance might, I suppose, be regarded as an expression of passionate and frank love, but the completely thoughtless way in which he put it on in front of me was of course bound to end in failure. It's not that I want people to be hypocritical and put on a show over love — it's just that I feel it's completely pointless to try to melt my heart by behaving like a little boy. Perhaps I was born with this hard heart. If so, I deserve the trouble and grief that all my ways of upsetting people have brought me.

After Wei had gone I naturally thought over my own feelings, and remembered in every detail the kindness, generosity, honesty and tenderness of someone else's manner. That alone was so marvellous that I was drunk on its heady sweetness and warmth. I wrote a few words on a card straight away and sent a porter round to Dormitory No. 4 with it at once.

9 March

When I saw Ling Jishi sitting so relaxed and casual in my room I couldn't help feeling sorry for Wei and praying that other women wouldn't be like me, neglecting and despising his admirable sincerity and falling into a vast misery from which I'll never be able to extricate myself. I hope even more strongly that a sincere and pure young woman will accept all of Wei's love and fill the emptiness he now feels.

13 March

I haven't written anything for several days. I don't know whether this is because I've been in such low spirits or because I can't find the so-called mood in which to write. All I know is that I've wanted to cry more than ever since yesterday. When people see me crying they think that it's because I'm homesick or worried about my illness. And when they see me smiling they think it's because I'm happy and enjoying the glow of returning health. Friends are all like that. Who can I tell about my infatuation that's not worth crying over but I haven't the strength to laugh about? Because I've seen the misery that the human passions and longings I won't give up have brought me, not even I am prepared to sympathise any longer with the grief that such blindness causes. Even less am I willing to take up my brush to write in detail about my self-blame and self-hatred.

Yes, I do seem to be having another moan. But this is just something hidden in my heart that I'm saying over and over to myself, which doesn't matter much. I've never had the courage to let people see my frowns and hear my sighs, even though I've long been groundlessly labelled "conceited", "eccentric" and the like. In fact I certainly don't want to moan, only to cry. If only there were someone who'd let me weep on his chest and tell him that I've ruined myself. But who can understand me, embrace me and comfort me? So all I can do is drown the words "I've ruined myself" in laughter.

Whatever am I trying to do? I can't say. Of course, I've never admitted to myself for a single moment that I'm in love with that tall man, but I can't put my finger on why he's in my every thought. His tall body, his tender pink face, his soft lips, and his charming eyes could allure a lot of women who were vulnerable to beauty, and his languid manner could bowl over any who were still capable of love. But why should I fall for a hundred-per-cent overseas Chinese just because of those meaningless charms? Really, I've found out from our latest conversations how pathetic his ideas are and what he wants: money, a young wife who would

know how to entertain his business friends in the draw-
ing room, and several fat, fair-skinned and very well-
dressed sons. What's his idea of love? Spending his
money in the whorehouse to buy a moment's physical
pleasure, or sitting on a well-upholstered settee with his
arms round a scented body, smoking a cigarette and
joking with his friends, his left leg folded on his right
knee. If he wasn't feeling very cheerful he'd forget
about it and go back home to his wife. His passions are
debates; tennis tournaments; going to study at Har-
vard; becoming a diplomat, an ambassador or a min-
ister; following in his father's professional footsteps;
going into the rubber business; becoming a capitalist.
. . . What ambitions! Apart from his resentment that
his father does not give him enough money, nothing can
stop him from sleeping soundly at night. If he has any
other complaints, it is only that as there are so few
good-looking women in Beijing he sometimes gets fed
up with going to theatres, cinemas and parks. What
can I say? I realized what a mean and low soul there
is in that noble and beautiful form I adore. And I've
accepted so much affection from him for no good reason at all. Of course, this affection isn't worth half of
what's left over from what he squanders in the brothels. When I think of how he kisses me on my hair
I want to cry from shame. Aren't I just offering myself
to him to trifle with as if I were one of the sisters who
sell themselves? But this only makes me feel more
guilty and wretched. If only, if only I'd been prepared
to give him a glare that showed I was really turning
him down I believe he'd never have been so bold, and
I also believe that the reason why is because he's never

been burned by the fires of love. I can't find the words to curse myself with.

14 March

Is this love? Perhaps only love can have such magic power. Why else should someone's thinking be so transformed and incalculable? When I went to sleep I despised that pretty boy, but the moment I woke up and opened my eyes I was thinking of that philistine and wondering if he'd be coming today, and when. Early in the morning? This afternoon? In the evening? Then I jumped out of bed, washed my face in a great hurry, made the bed, picked up the big book that was dropped on the floor last night and kept rubbing its edges. It's a volume of speeches by President Wilson that Ling Jishi forgot and left here last night.

14 March, evening

I have such a beautiful dream that Ling Jishi gave me. But he's also ruined it. It's only because of him that I can drink the pure wine of youth to the full, and spend the morning in the smile of love. But it's also because of him that I've come to understand this thing called "life", been disappointed, wanted to die, and so detested my own willingness to fall that the punishment I've brought on myself has seemed the lightest possible. Truly, sometimes I've even wondered if I'd have the strength to kill someone to preserve what I love.

I've thought it over. I reckon that in order to preserve my beautiful dreams and to prevent my life-force ebbing away day by day the best thing would be to go to the Western Hills at once. But Yufang tells me that the friend of hers who lives in the Western Hills she's asked to find me a house there hasn't answered her letter yet. There's no way I can make enquiries myself or hurry things along. But I've made my mind up. I've decided to let that tall swine have a taste of me being disobliging. I'm going to be heartlessly arrogant and insulting.

17 March

After storming off in such a bad temper the other night Wei came back all meek and mild today to make his peace with me. I couldn't help laughing, but I also realized how lovable he is. A woman who wants a faithful husband for the rest of her life couldn't possibly find a more reliable one than Wei. "Are you still angry with me, Wei?" I asked him with a smile. "No, sister, I'd never dare," he replied, all embarrassed. "You understand me. My only thought is the hope you won't ditch me. All I want is for things to go well for you. If you're happy that's enough for me." So sincere, so moving. What a comparison with that fair-skinned face and red lips. But later on I said, "Wei, you're fine. One day everything will come out right for you." He gave a bitter smile. "Never. But I wish you were right." What did he mean? He was making things hard for me again. I longed to be able to kneel down in front of him and beg him to love me as a friend or younger brother would. For purely selfish reasons I want fewer complications and more happiness. Wei loves me and can say all those nice things, but there are two things he forgets: first, he should damp down his passion; and second, he should conceal his love. I feel unbearably apologetic about being unable to do anything for that honest man.

18 March

I've asked Xia too to look for a house for me in the Western Hills.

19 March

Ling Jishi hasn't been here for several days. Of course, I don't know how to dress, I'm useless at social behaviour, I'm no good at household management, I've got T.B. and I'm broke, so what would he want to come here for? I didn't want him to come, but when he stayed away it made me feel more miserable than ever and was even more proof of his earlier frivolity. It can't be because he's as well-behaved as Wei. When he got my note — "I'm ill, so please don't come and disturb me" — could he have believed I meant it and not come because he didn't want to disobey me? So now I want to see him again to find out just how that monster sees me.

20 March

I went to see Yunlin three times today, but didn't meet the man I wanted to meet. Yunlin seemed a bit puzzled and asked me if I'd seen Ling Jishi during the last few days. All I could do was come back in misery. I really am very anxious, and I can't kid myself that I haven't been thinking of him these last few days.

Yufang and Yunlin came at seven this evening to ask me to the Third Campus to listen to an English debate. Ling Jishi was the captain of one of the teams. The moment I heard this news my heart began to pound. I had to use my illness as the excuse for turning down this well-meant invitation. I'm hopelessly weak. I didn't have the courage to undergo an emotional upheaval. I was still hoping I'd be able to avoid seeing him. But as they left I asked them to give Ling Jishi my regards and tell him I'd asked after him. What a stupid thing to do!

21 March

I'd just drunk my egg and milk when there was a familiar knock at the door and a tall shadow could be seen through the paper window. All I wanted to do was to leap up and open the door. I don't know what emotion it was that helped me to control myself and keep my head down.

"Are you out of bed yet, Sophie?" The voice was so tender that I could have burst into tears.

Was it to know that I was already in my chair or to know that I didn't have it in me to lose my temper and reject him that he pushed the door quietly open and came in? I didn't dare raise my damp eyelids.

"Are you any better? Have you just got up?"

I said not a word in reply.

"You're very angry with me. You're sick of me, Sophie. I'd better go."

That would have been best for me, but I jerked my head up and gave him a look that stopped his hand from opening the door.

Who says he's not a bad lot? He understood me and dared to hold both my hands tight.

"Sophie," he said, "you've treated me badly. I've not dared come in when I pass your door every day.

I wouldn't have dared come today if Yunlin hadn't told me you wouldn't be angry with me. Are you tired of me, Sophie?"

Anyone could have realized that if he'd dared embrace and kiss me wildly I'd have laid my head on his wrist and wept, "I love you, I love you." But he was cold, so cold that he made me start hating him again. Then I thought in my heart, "Come here, embrace me, I want to kiss your face." Of course, he was still holding my hands and gazing fixedly at my face. But when I looked hard at every expression of his feelings I could find no sign of what I wanted him to give me. Why does he only understand what's useless and contemptible about me? Why can't he see his place in my heart? I wished I could kick him out, but I was in the grip of another emotion. I shook my head to show him that I was not cross with him for coming.

Then I meekly accepted all kinds of shallow marks of affection from him, listened to him talking with such relish about his trivial pleasures and his view that earning and spending money was the meaning of life, and let him give me a lot of hints about how women should behave. This made me despise him, curse him under my breath, jeer at him, and secretly hit my heart hard with my fist. But when he strode out of my room I felt so wretched that I wanted to cry. Because I controlled my raging desires I didn't ask him to stay a little longer.

He went, alas.

21 March, night

What a life I was living this time last year. I used to stay in bed pretending to be ill and refusing to get up to make Yun care for me and do just what I wanted. To make her caress me I exploited the desperate and unconsolable tears that flowed when I laid my head on the table, thinking of trivial upsets and sobbing aloud. Sometimes I'd be feeling rather sad after a whole day of silent thought, and this pale melancholy would make me more eager than ever to stir up that sort of emotion. It was almost as if I could taste a little sweetness that way. Now I can't even bear to think of listening to Yun lying on the grass in the French park at night and singing *The Peony Pavilion*. If she hadn't been tricked by God into loving that pasty-faced man she'd never have died so early and of course I'd never have drifted to Beijing by myself to struggle against disease without relatives or love. Although I've got several friends and they're very sorry for me, can my relationship with them be set on the scales against the love between me and Yun? When I think of Yun I really ought to let go and weep aloud the way I used to when I was acting the spoiled child for her. But this last year I've learnt too much. Although I often want to cry I choke it back because I'm afraid that people would dislike it if they knew about it. I've even less idea why all I can do at the moment is feel anxious. I can't find the little bit of calm I want in which to consider the good and bad effects of what I do and think on my health, my reputation and my future. All day my disordered brain thinks about what I don't want it to think about. It's precisely what I want to avoid that makes me more and more indescribably upset and miserable. But now I have nothing else to hope for. I can only say, "Death would serve me right."

Could I find any sympathy or consolation? But then I just seem to be begging for pity.

Yufang and Yunlin came here after supper, and at 9 I still wouldn't let them go. I knew that Yufang made herself sit down again so as not to hurt my feelings, but Yunlin insisted on going back by himself on the excuse that he had to prepare for classes tomorrow. I hinted at the dilemma I've been in recently to Yufang, longing for her to be able to understand, to take the initiative, change my life and do what I'm not up to doing. But she took what I said the wrong way and faithfully warned me, "Sophie, you're not being fair to him. Of course, you don't do it deliberately, but you ought to be more careful about the way you look at people. You must realize that Ling Jishi and his friends aren't like the boys who used to go out with us in Shanghai. They see very little of women and can't resist a spot of kindness. You mustn't cause him despair and pain in the future. I realize you couldn't possibly love him." Is this my fault too? If I'd not talked freely to her to ask her help would she have said these things that made me even more angry and upset? I swallowed my temper and smiled. "Don't make me sound too awful, Yufang," I said.

When she offered to spend the night here I sent her home.

When brilliant women are feeling a bit miserable they can write lots of classical or modern poems about their "grief and emotion" or the "sorrows of the heart". But I'm useless. I'm in this poetic situation but I can't make anything of it. I can't even use tears as an alternative to poetry to express my emotional turmoil.

For this reason alone I ought to drop everything and live for all I'm worth if I'm not to fall behind others. At the very least I ought to be able to use a pen or a gun for my own amusement and the admiration of a crowd of shallow eyes. Really, I've dropped myself into misery that's worse than death, and all just for that man's soft hair and red lips.

I dreamt of a man with the manner of a mediaeval European knight. Anyone who's seen Ling Jishi would realize how appropriate the comparison is. He combines it with the special gentleness of the East. God generously gave him everything else that's good, but why did he leave out all intelligence? He doesn't understand what real love is, he really doesn't, even though he already has a wife (Yufang told me that tonight), even though he once cycled after a woman in a rickshaw in Singapore and loved her for a little while after, even though he used to spend the night in the Hanjiatan brothels. But has he ever been loved by a woman? Has he ever loved a woman? I'm sure he hasn't.

A strange idea has been burning in my head again. I've decided to educate that student. The universe isn't as simple as he imagines it to be.

22 March

My mind's in turmoil, but I've forced myself to write this diary. I started it because Yun kept on asking me to in letters, over and over again. Although Yun has been dead for a long time now I couldn't bear to give up writing it. I suppose it must be that because of the very serious advice she gave me when she was alive I want to go on writing it for ever in her memory. So no matter how little I feel like writing I force myself to scribble half a page or so. I was already in bed, but the sight of Yun's picture on the wall was more than I could bear. I dragged myself out of bed and started writing this to spare myself the agony of yearning for her. Of course, the only person I'd ever have shown this diary to was Yun. First, because I only record all these trivial details as Yun wanted to know about my life, and second because I don't want people to show in their faces that they know too much when they look at me — that would be even more wounding. It seems that I really feel guilty and miserable because of the morality that other people respect. So I've long kept this black notebook at the bottom of the mattress under my pillow.

Today, alas, I forgot my old intention. I did so because I had to, unconsidered though my action may have appeared. Recently Wei has been misunderstanding me completely. This often makes him feel very uneasy, which then affects me. I'm sure that everything I do shows what my attitude is. Why can't he realize what I'm trying to say to him? But I couldn't tell him directly to stop him loving me. I often think that if it had been anyone else but Wei I'd have known the best way to deal with him. But Wei would have to be so good a man — I can't bring myself to do it. So there was nothing for it but to show him my diary. I let him see that there's no hope for him in my heart and that I'm a cold and fickle woman not worth loving. If Wei understood me he would of course become the only friend I could pour out my heart to. I'd hug him and kiss him warmly, and hope that he'd find the most lovable and beautiful woman in the world. Wei read the diary through then read it again. He cried, but he was extraordinarily calm. I was astonished.

"Do you understand me?" I asked.

He nodded.

"Do you believe me now?"

"About what?"

Only then did I realize what his nod meant. Anyone who can really understand me will understand this diary that can express only a ten-thousandth part of me, this diary that only causes me the misery of seeing how limited it is. Besides, it's depressing enough in itself to try to get others to understand me and to show someone a diary that uses all sorts of devices to explain things over and over again. On top of that Wei was worried afterwards that I'd think he hadn't understood me.

"You love him," he kept saying, "you love him. I'm not good enough for you."

I'd have torn the diary up in a fury. I couldn't deny that I'd sullied it. All I could say to Wei was, "I want to go to bed. Come back tomorrow."

Never hope for anything from others. Isn't this appalling? If my dear Yun were still alive to read my diary I know she'd have embraced me, wept and said, "Sophie, my Sophie, why can't I be a bit greater so as to spare my Sophie all this grief?" But Yun is dead. If only I could weep bitterly with this diary in my hands.

23 March

"Sophie," Ling Jishi said to me, "you really are a strange girl." I can understand that gasp of completely incomprehending admiration. Why he finds me strange is because he can see my tattered gloves, the chest of drawers in which no perfume is to be found, the new quilted dress torn to shreds for no good reason at all, the old toys I've kept. Any other reason? He's heard some strange laughs from me. There's no way in which he could appreciate anything else, as I've never said anything to him that really comes from me. For example, I smile when he says, "From now on I'm going to try hard to earn some money." When he told me about arranging to meet his friends to chase women students in the park — "It's real fun, Sophie" — I smiled too. Of course, what he means by strange is something he's not used to in his ordinary life. It depresses me that there's no way I can make him understand and respect me. My only wish now is to go to the Western Hills. When I think of all the wild illusions I used to have I find them ridiculous.

24 March

When he's alone with me and I gaze at that face and hear that voice like music my heart has to endure emotional torture. Why don't I fling myself at him to kiss his lips, his brow and all the rest of him? Really, sometimes I'm on the point of saying, "My king! Let me kiss you!" The reason — no, not reason, because I've never had any sense of reason, but some other feeling of self-respect — keeps me under control and holds the words back. No matter how dreadful his ideas are, there's no doubt that he drives my emotions wild. So why don't I admit I'm in love with him? I'm certain that if he were to hold me in a close embrace and let me kiss him all over then throw me into the sea or a fire I'd gladly shut my eyes to greet the death that would preserve my love for ever. I have fallen in love with him: it'll be enough for me if he gives me a good death.

24 March, late at night

I've made my mind up. To save myself from being dragged down by a sexual obsession I'm going to Xia's tomorrow morning. I'll avoid the agony of seeing Ling Jishi. This agony has been tormenting me for so long.

26 March

I left here because of one entanglement but then another one forced me to rush straight back. The day after I got to Xia's Mengru turned up too. Although she said she'd come to see someone else it hurt me very much. She went on and on that night about some new theory of the emotions she'd just picked up, indirectly getting at me. I kept quiet to deny her any further satisfaction. I lay wide awake all night in Xia's bed till dawn then came straight back here, still having to contain my fury.

Yufang told me that she's found a house in the Western Hills and another companion for me. She's an invalid too, and a good friend of Yufang's. I ought to be very happy at the news, but no sooner had the frown begun to disappear from my forehead when a kind of silent desolation fell on it again. Although I left home as a child and have been around in the world since then, I've always had friends or relations with me. Going to the Western Hills will only take me a few miles from town, but it'll be the first time in all my twenty years I've ever gone to a strange place by myself. If I quietly die in those hills who'll discover my body? Can I be sure I won't die there? Perhaps some people would think me ridiculous for worrying over such trivialities but they really have made me cry. When I asked Yufang if she'd miss me she laughed at me for asking so childish a question. She said that it was so near she wouldn't be losing me. I could only wipe away my tears with embarrassment when she promised to visit me in the hills every week.

I went to Wei's in the afternoon. He too promised to visit me in the hills every week on days Yufang doesn't go.

By the time I came back it was late. I cried again packing my things all by myself and thinking how I'd be leaving all my friends in Beijing. When I realized that none of them had ever cried to me I dried my tears. Once again I've decided to leave this ancient city alone and by myself.

In my loneliness I thought of Ling Jishi again. In fact it's not true to say of Ling Jishi that I've thought of him or thought of him again. I'm obsessed with him all day long. What I should say is that I'm going to talk about my Ling Jishi again. The separation I've been deliberately arranging these last few days will be an incalculable loss for me. I wanted to let him go, but I've only been clinging to him more tightly than ever. As I can't pluck him right out of my heart why do I keep avoiding seeing him face to face? I'm really upset. I can't leave him like this and go to the Western Hills feeling so lonely.

27 March

Early this morning Yufang went to the Western Hills to fix up my house for me. She said I can go tomorrow.

How can I find the non-existent words to express my gratitude for her great kindness? I'd have preferred to spend another day in town, but I could hardly say so.

Ling Jishi only came when I was feeling very anxious. I grasped both his hands tightly.

"Sophie," he said, "I haven't seen you for days."

I wished I could have wept then with my arms around him, but all I could do was smile again and keep the tears back.   Hearing that I'm going to the Western Hills tomorrow, he showed a kind of astonishment and sighed, which was a big consolation for me, so my smile became a real one.   When he saw my smile he clutched my hands so tight that they hurt.

"You're smiling, you're smiling," he said.   He seemed to be angry.   The pain was more delicious than anything I've known before.   It was as if something were boring into my heart. Just when I wanted to fall into his arms Wei arrived.

Wei knew I was angry with him for coming, but he just wouldn't leave.   I gave Ling Jishi a look and said, "Have you got a class now?"   Then I saw Ling Jishi out.   He asked me when I was leaving tomorrow and I told him.   When I asked him if he'd come back he said he'd do so very soon.   I gazed at him with delight, forgetting how contemptible his character is and how he only looks beautiful.   Just then he was a lover out of a romance in my eyes. Yes, Sophie has a lover!

27 March, late

It's been five whole hours since I saw Wei off.   How can I find the right words to describe these five hours?

I've been as restless in this little room as an ant in a hot pan, sitting down, standing up again, and rushing to the door to peep outside, but — he's definitely not coming, he's definitely not coming. I wanted to cry again at the dreariness of my departure. Is there nobody in all Beijing who will cry with me? Yes, I ought to leave this cruel city, so why am I so attached to this plank bed, this greasy desk, this three-legged chair? Yes, I'm going tomorrow morning, and my Beijing friends won't have to be fed up with Sophie any longer. For the sake of her friends' happiness and comfort Sophie ought to die in the Western Hills. But they are all prepared to let Sophie go off to the hills lonely and by herself without a touch of warmth. Presumably Sophie won't die, and people won't suffer any loss or be emotionally disturbed. . . . No, I don't want to think any more. No. Why should I want to? If Sophie weren't so greedy to wallow in emotions wouldn't she be satisfied with those sympathetic looks?

As for friends, I'll say nothing. I know that Sophie will never be satisfied with human friendship.

But where else can I find satisfaction? Ling Jishi promised me he'd come, but it's already 9. Even if he did come would it make me happy? Could he give me what I need?

Now I realize that he's not coming I ought to hate myself. Long, long ago I used to know the right attitude towards different kinds of men, but I've turned stupid now. Why did I give him that imploring look when I asked him if he'd be coming back? I shouldn't be so open with so handsome a man and make myself look cheap. But I love him. Why should I use tricks?

Can't I express my love to him directly? It seems to me that there's no reason why I shou'dn't be allowed to give him a hundred kisses provided nobody else is harmed.

By promising to come and breaking his word he's shown that he's only trifling with me. My friend, you won't lose anything by showing Sophie some goodwill when she's leaving.

Tonight I've gone completely crazy. At a time like this language and words seem so useless. My heart feels as if it's being gnawed by hordes of mice, or as if a brazier were burning inside it. If only I could smash everything or rush wildly out into the night. I can't control the surges of wild emotion, and I lie on this bed of nails of passion, which drive themselves into me whichever way I turn. Then I seem to be in a cauldron of oil listening to it bubbling and boiling as my whole body is scalded. Why don't I run out? I'm waiting for a vague and meaningless hope to be realized. Oh. . . . At the thought of those red lips I've gone crazy again. If this hope were possible — I couldn't help laughing by myself. I asked myself over and over again, "Do you love him?" And then I laughed even more. Sophie couldn't be so stupid as to love that overseas Chinese that much. Surely I can't be forbidden to do something that does nobody else a scrap of harm just because I won't admit I love him.

If he's really not coming tonight how can I bring myself to go off to the Western Hills as if I didn't give a damn?

Oh dear! It's 9:30.

9:40.

28 March, 3 a.m.

All her life Sophie has been too passionate and too sincere about wanting people to understand her and share her feelings. That's why she's been submerged in bitter disappointment for so long. But who else, apart from her, can know the weight of her tears?

This diary is less a record of Sophie's life than simply every one of those tears. Only they seem true to her. But this diary is now coming to an end because Sophie no longer needs to give vent to her resentment and find consolation through tears. This is because I feel that everything is meaningless, and that tears are the profoundest expression of this meaninglessness. But on the last page of this diary Sophie should happily celebrate finding satisfaction in the depths of her despair, satisfaction that ought to kill her with happiness. Yet all I find in this satisfaction is a sense of victory, a victory in which I find desolation and an even deeper sense of how pathetic and ridiculous I am. So the "beauty" I've been dreaming about so obsessively for months — that tall man's elegance — has now faded far away.

How can I explain the psychology of a woman who's crazy about a man's looks? Of course I could never love him, and the reason is easily explained: such a low and ugly soul lurks behind his beauty. But I admire him, long for him, and without him I'll lose everything that ensures my life's meaning. I always thought that if one day our lips were to join close, close together I'd cheerfully let my body go to pieces with the wild joy of my heart. Indeed, I'd have sacrificed everything just for a caress from that knight of a man and the casual touch of his fingertips anywhere on my body.

I ought to be going wild because I've had all the amazing dreamlike things in my fantasies happen to me without any difficulty at all. But did it all give me the soul-intoxicating bliss I'd imagined? No.

When he, Ling Jishi, came at ten last night he started trying to tell me in his clumsy way how he longed for me. My heart was touched many times. But when I saw his eyes burning with sexual desire I was frightened. The oaths he swore, that were even uglier than the low mentality from which they sprang, revived my self-respect. I'm sure that if he'd given all that superficial, nauseating sweet talk to other women they'd have found it very delightful and he'd have won a so-called loving heart. But when he spoke to me the force of all those words only pushed me even further away from him. Poor man! Although God gave you so beautiful a body at the same time he tricked you by crowning your life with so totally ill-matched a soul. Do you imagine that what I long for is "family" and "money"? That I'd be proud of social position? "What a pathetic man you look to me!" Just when I was wishing I could weep for his misfortune he was still staring at my face with that terrifying, burning lust. If all he'd wanted had been physical satisfaction his beauty would have overwhelmed my heart, but he said in that weepy voice, "Believe me, Sophie, I'll never let you down." Pathetic man. He didn't realise with what contempt the woman in front of him pitied him for that kind of performance and for that sort of remark. I couldn't help laughing aloud. To say that he knew what love is and could love me is almost a joke. Weren't his two flashing eyes, burning with lust, proclaiming that he knew about nothing except despicable and shallow needs?

"Hey, be sensible and clear off. Hanjiatan's the place for you to look for your pleasures." As I'd seen through him that's what I should have said, and sent that lowest of human beings packing. But although I was secretly mocking him I forgot about everything when he boldly and rapidly put his arms round me. I temporarily lost my self-respect and pride, completely bewitched by the charm that's the only thing he has. In my heart all I could think was, "Tighter. Longer. I'm leaving tomorrow." If I'd had any self-control then I'd have thought of the other things besides his beauty and thrown him outside like a stone.

Oh dear! What kind of words or emotions should I repent with? You, Ling Jishi, a man as contemptible as you, kissed me. And meekly and quietly I let you. But when that warm, moist soft thing was on my face what was my heart getting? I would never swoon like some women in the arms of their lovers. I was looking at him, my eyes wide open, thinking, "I've won! I've won!" It was because when he kissed me I knew the taste of what it was that bewitched me, and at the same time I despised myself. That's why I suddenly felt miserable, pushed him away and started crying.

Perhaps he paid no attention to my tears and thought that his lips had given me such warmth, softness and tenderness that my heart was too intoxicated to know what it was doing. That was why he sat down beside me again and went on saying a lot of nauseating things that are supposed to be expressions of love.

"Why do you have to expose all your appalling side?" I really began to feel sorry for him again.

"Don't you get any wild ideas," I said. "I might be dead tomorrow."

Goodness only knows what impact my words had on him. He kissed me again but I evaded him, and his lips landed on my hand.

My mind was made up. My mind was clear enough for me to insist that he went. He looked rather disgruntled and wouldn't leave me alone. "Why are you being so stubborn?" I wondered. He didn't go till 12:30 a.m.

When he'd left I thought about what had just happened. I wanted to hit my heart hard, with all my strength. Why did I let a man I despise so much kiss me? I don't love him and I was jeering at him, but why did I let him embrace me? Really it was just because he looks like a knight that I feel so low.

In short, I've ruined myself. How in heaven's name am I going to avenge and make up for all my losses when I'm my own enemy?

Fortunately my life is mine alone in all the universe to play with. I've already wasted enough of it. It doesn't seem to be a matter of any importance that this experience has thrown me into the very depths of grief.

But I refuse to stay in Beijing, let alone go to the Western Hills. I've decided to take the train south to waste what's left of my life where nobody knows me, and as a result my wounded heart has perked up. I'm laughing wildly with self-pity.

"Quietly go on living, and quietly die. I'm sorry for you, Sophie."   1928

Shanghai in the Spring of 1930 (2)

IN the early spring dawn a moist breeze lightly blew in through the broken glass of the window, gently brushed over everything and quietly slipped away. The pale light of the sky had filled every corner and coloured the whole room like a dream. It was too early for the city's noise and an ideal time for sleep, but Wangwei, who had stayed awake till very late, woke with a start. Opening his tired, bleary eyes he gazed vacantly at the sky for a while then shut his eyes again as if he had not a care in the world, rolled over, and drifted back to sleep. He was an attractive, brown-skinned young man. No sooner had his eyelids closed than a beautiful image sprang up in his mind, whereupon he turned over again as if with alarm and sat up. As if he could hardly believe it, he took the simple telegram out from under his pillow and read it again:

SAILING TODAY SS DAIRENMARU ARRIVING SHANGHAI MORNING AFTER NEXT PLEASE MEET DOCKSIDE

The brown face glowed with happiness. He rubbed the bristles on his chin then grinned more broadly, repeating to himself as he put on his old black flannel trousers:

"Funny girl. She wrote no letters while I expected them, then just when I'm being worked off my feet she decides to come herself. You really are a strange one, Mary."

As he said her lovely name he couldn't help looking rather pleased with himself.

He gave his face a quick wash in cold water then rushed along the misty street towards the Bund.

The street was very quiet. There was only the occasional horse-drawn rubbish cart and a few dejected street-sweepers. Here and there one or two sleepy apprentices, their eyes only half open, were taking down the shutters of their shops. The ground was all wet with the mist, which spread its thin, pale, cloudy whiteness everywhere. The air was cold and pleasant. Wangwei walked to the tram stop, waited for a while then took a tram to the Bund. The noise of the iron wheels was even more ear-shattering than usual in this silent boundless space, and the tram seemed to be jolting even more than usual. Not that he noticed any of this: he was oblivious to all else as his gaze was fixed on the fog in front of him, a white fog in which that bewitching, delicate flower of a face kept appearing.

He had met her at an unimportant banquet during the previous year's summer vacation. She had not paid any attention to him at the time. She had talked a lot, been very lively, conspicuously drunk a great deal, and scarcely looked at him. He did not know why, but her proud and free ways, her charming insolence, had particularly captivated him. Seeing her insouciant brow with its occasional hint of a frown he had been sure that she must be extremely lonely, and lonely in

a way that most people could not understand. This
had made him feel somehow even closer to her. When
he heard her laughing he found to his surprise that
she made his heart tremble. The next day he had boldly called on her and been made very welcome. A few
days later she had gone to Beiping to study. He had
not dared to believe that any strong friendship had
been built up between them. In those days he was
something of a pessimist anyhow, and from then on
he had been in even lower spirits. But later an off
and on correspondence had given rise to a very disturbing hunch and strengthened his most extravagant
hopes. Crushed by pain, he had gone straight to Beiping.

In the end they had lived together just as they
wanted for a while, then gone back south together.
This had been during the winter vacation, and she had
insisted on leaving him to go home. Their agreement
had been that she would return to Shanghai after the
traditional New Year, but she had not kept it. Only
much later had she sent him a short letter from Beiping, giving not a shred of explanation but asking him
to forgive her. He had been most upset and had almost fallen back into the depths of misery. But at the
same time a new hope had been egging him on. He
was by now deeply interested in contemporary politics
and economics, reading many books voraciously and
closely, and gradually becoming involved in practical
struggles. Although he kept on writing to her, thinking
of her, and regretting his loss of her he had not had
much time for it. The letters had gradually become
shorter, and he had stopped missing her so profound-
ly. Sometimes he had forgotten about her for days on

end. This had not been by choice. Her beautiful image was in fact buried very deeply in his heart. It consoled him when he was exhausted and unhappy. Only he knew how much he loved her. The sudden arrival of her telegram the day before had filled him again with hopes and dreams. All the sweetness of the past had come back to him, and he longed to see her. There was so much he wanted to tell her, especially about the work he had been doing recently.

The tram soon reached the Bund.

Many large boats on the Huangpu River were preparing to raise anchor amid an endless clanking of chains and the sound of strident and powerful hooters. Little sampans in midstream were rowing workers across the river. The sun was up now. Warm, pale yellow light was streaming across from the other side of the river, stretching long, thin shadows across the tarmac of the road. Wangwei took a deep breath of the morning air. His excited face kept rubbing against the cool breeze. He felt very relaxed and had a great sense of well-being. It was as though his whole body were full of something just waiting to explode. Quietly and hastily he was searching for the NYK dock.

He found the dock, but to his surprise it was deserted: all that could be seen was an expanse of river. No boat was moored there. As he gazed distractedly out at the river he had not known whether he was too early or too late. He was much afraid that Mary had only sent the cable as a joke on him. It would have been quite within her character and tastes to have played so cruel a trick: she often did things just to satisfy a passing whim. He could not think what to do before finally deciding to go to the shipping office and make enquires.

The office told him that the boat would not dock before 2:30 that afternoon. He then dragged himself weakly back home, as if he had now found new hope.

After eating he went to sit in a room for a couple of hours, translating English newspapers into Chinese and Chinese ones into English. Sometimes he had to take documents to another office. There were often meetings to discuss the society's business or theoretical problems, as well as detailed considerations of whether or not the current political line was correct. All this frequently kept him so busy that it was midnight before he could go home. Sometimes he would not even be able to take the next morning off as he often had to draft outline plans, organizational outlines, manifestos, bulletins and the like. He had gone short of sleep for many nights on end, which was why he looked so dog-tired as he went to the place where he worked.

The room, which looked like a clerk's office, was the temporary office of the — society, an association set up under the guidance of —.* It was a body involved in the proletarian literary movement run by a number of worker intellectuals. As such a body could not function openly under the existing government the sign outside the room proclaimed it to be an embroidery company. There were a few of them who did the work there, and young Wangwei, who never came late

---

* These blanks, and some later in the story, were left in the original to evade Kuomintang censorship. Readers at the time would have taken these gaps as referring to the Communist Party and related organizations. — *Tr.*

or missed a day, was the most trusted of them. When he arrived today he found not only the cleaner but also the short secretary Feng Fei. Feng was often late as he lived quite far away, so Wangwei was a little shocked to find him sitting alone there casually smoking. "Oh, good morning, Feng."

"Mmm. . . ."

There was a flash of brightness in Feng's rather flat face that Wangwei had hardly ever seen before, so Wangwei asked him, "What's making you so cheerful?"

"Nothing. . . ." Feng was in fact thinking about a very lucky encounter. A month earlier he had come to know a tram conductress by sight, but had never had the chance to speak to her. He had been able to see her at a set time every day, and every time his respect for her had grown. She dressed very simply and never wore a spot of make-up, but she was so capable and her cheeks so smooth and pink, a healthy colour that her work and her enthusiasm had given them. From her manner and the way she spoke (she often expressed her views forcefully in arguments with passengers over one thing or other) he could tell for certain that she had some education, the wisdom of her class and a simple but correct understanding of politics. He had often wanted to speak to her as he felt he already knew her very well, but his customary timidity always made him miss his chances. He had set out a little early today because he had something else to do, and was standing at the bus stop with his head buried in a tabloid newspaper when he heard a voice. When he looked round, who had it been but that conductress standing behind him and giving him an open smile?

He had felt rather awkward, but she had said to him:

"Hey, you're out a bit earlier than usual today, aren't you?"

"Mmm . . . Yes . . ." had been his reply.

"I'm rushed off my feet today," she had continued. "I've got to stand in for a mate. I won't get a moment's break today. She's ill, but she can't ask for time off, and in the evening I've got to buy her medicine for her too. Where do you work, sir?"

"I've got a job in a company."

She had looked him up and down and shook her head as she replied with a smile, "You don't look the part. You look more like a student. I'm very good at telling what people really are."

By the time they had exchanged a few more words the tram arrived. She had lightly sprung aboard, greeted another conductress, and taken the ticket-holder and the canvas money-bag from her. When he got off the tram Feng had been able to say goodbye to her in the most natural way, just as if to an old friend.

He was thinking about all this again now. He had had very little contact with women and had disliked the run of young ladies at university. This conductress was the first woman he had ever really paid any attention to. He made all sorts of guesses about her, and made up a brilliant and moving life story for her. Hence Feng's failure to notice that Wangwei had shaved, and that although he said he was very tired his face showed more clearly than anyone else's would have done that something very happy was about to happen to him.

That day Wangwei left work a little earlier than

usual, also missing a meeting. At last he met a beautiful woman on the boat and took her home with her several pieces of luggage.

2

As the sedan drove down the broad Avenue Edouard VII Wangwei held a soft little hand. They gazed at each other with wordless smiles, not knowing in their happiness what to say first. After a long silence she said, "How have you been looking after yourself recently? You look a lot thinner."

Rubbing his newly shaved cheeks, he replied with a smile, "I thought I'd better look a bit more presentable today." At the thought of his whiskers, which had been growing much more vigorously recently, he smiled again and was on the point of telling her about them then decided not to. He would let her notice them on his face in her own time. "You're lovelier than ever, Mary," he said, squeezing her hand.

He lifted the delicate hand to his lips. She moved a little closer to him.

With a sign of happiness and an adoring gaze he said, "Never leave me again, Mary."

She turned her face towards him in a most captivating way, and two pairs of lips that had been longing for each other joined in a passionate kiss. They kissed hard, as if they were drunk or faint, as they held each other with arms drained of strength, oblivious of everything else.

As the taxi made a sharp turn, shaking violently, they remembered themselves and drew apart. He hastily put his hand out to steady the little case that had been jolted hard. In the front mirror he could see that the driver couldn't control his laughter. He felt a touch of anger and embarrassment, but all he could do was smile at the wicked grin in the driving mirror.

When they reached his place the pair of them sprang happily out of the taxi. He made four trips from the taxi up to the second floor through the little back door. Cases and bedding were piled up beside the staircase, and as he fished his key out of his pocket to open the door he looked at Mary and said, "This room may be a little small for the two of us. We can move later."

The room really was small, and very simply furnished with a bed, a table, a couple of chairs, a bookcase and a wardrobe. As there were so few things in it it did not seem so very small, only rather low-ceilinged and a little stuffy. As he spent little time there, and most of that asleep, he had not noticed. But Mary, who had just spent two days at sea, felt it straight away. She did not say anything about it, but praised him for keeping it so clean.

"It's all thanks to the landlady," he explained. "She keeps everything tidy for me. The furniture's hers too. I even get my tea from her. The reason why I live here is because I like having everything so convenient. Yes, I'll go and ask her for some hot water."

But Mary stopped him, looked at the watch on her wrist, saw that it was nearly five, and asked, "How do you eat normally?"

"It depends. At different times and different places. Are you hungry?"

"Starving. I had some rice porridge for breakfast,

but I was too excited to be able to eat any lunch. We'll have to get some food inside us before we can do anything else."

"Right." He picked up his hat, ready to go.

"Where are we going?" she asked. "Where do you usually eat?"

As he thought of all those dirty, crowded little eating places and looked at her imported fur-trimmed silk coat, clean gloves and shiny, openwork shoes he burst out laughing. "You couldn't go to any of those places, Mary. I've come down in the world recently. Today I owe you a welcome banquet, so let's go somewhere good. We can work out a long-term solution tomorrow. Where would you like to go?"

"Are you taking me out?" Mary asked with a charming smile. "How much money have you got with you?"

He reckoned that he ought to have about four dollars left in his pocket, and that if they chose carefully it ought to be enough. Mary liked Cantonese cooking, so they took a long ride in a rickshaw.

They ate very well, and took their time over the meal. As Mary was feeling so happy she did not hold back any of her beauty, and kept acting rather boldly and flirtatiously, which made her more bewitching than ever. By then she had taken off her 120-dollar coat, and was wearing only a close-fitting cheongsam in flimsy, bright green satin, so that her charms were half hidden and half revealed by her dress. She told him all sorts of funny stories about how much she had missed him, she told him that she would never be able to leave him again, and she explained why she had let him down before. Although she said he would be able to forgive her, she'd been punished for it twice over. Her life in Beiping recently had been quite miserable, but she hadn't wanted to let on to anyone. She hadn't even understood why herself. She said that she wanted him to be the only person in the world who knew about it, and a bit of extra love from him would more than make up for it. What she said was all very affecting, and even if she did seem to be laying it on a little thick her efforts left him feeling rather upset on her account. The pressure of physical instinct made him ache to crush her under his weight and taste the intoxication of her beautiful body once again. He had no need of words to express his love.

"Let's finish the meal quickly," he kept saying.

She was not thinking along the same lines as him. She found the atmosphere in the restaurant stimulating. The red light that was shining on them both made him look rather more handsome. He was a reserved, strong man, while she felt a little feverish. She believed that this made her even more attractive, and the sweet wine and strong tea she kept swallowing increased her excitement. She was sitting on a soft seat with the man she loved and saying things that intoxicated him more than ever. Everything else had been forgotten except the way they were gradually inflaming each other, stirring up hearts that were already on fire. She really wanted to prolong this overwhelming emotion; she did not want to leave. She was afraid of going back and shattering this mood. That place was so cold, and there were so many tiresome jobs waiting to be done there. Her luggage was still piled up in the middle of the floor. Slowly she went on drinking.

Wangwei gradually fell silent. Before this he had been suffering from a loving desire that could not find fulfilment, holding himself back, and feeling his whole body burning. His eyes were bloodshot and almost on fire. He could only keep quiet and try not to listen to what she was saying. He was resisting her attraction because it gave him more pain than pleasure. He tried to concentrate on other things of no importance in order to alleviate his unbearable longing. So he kept quiet, pretending to listen to her while his thoughts were gradually moving elsewhere to many other detailed matters.

He deserved to be forgiven for this. Mary did not yet understand the pain a young man feels in the presence of the beautiful woman he loves.

The big clock in the restaurant struck seven, giving Wangwei a start. He remembered the meeting he had to go to that evening at 7:30. There would be nearly twenty people waiting for him, the chairman. He hesitated as he gazed at the lovely woman, not knowing what to do. He really did have to go to the meeting, and even if he left at once he was worried that he would be late. But could he? How could he leave Mary by herself in the restaurant? In his great impatience he shouted at the waiter with a touch of anger, "Hurry up with that rice!"

Mary did not take her eyes off him and said, as bewitchingly as ever, "Very well then. Let's have our rice and finish the meal."

After hastily swallowing his rice he stood up to leave. Mary, who had not yet put on her coat, did not show her irritation as she followed him out into the street without saying a word. They jumped into a couple of rickshaws and went back home as quickly as they could. She felt an irritation but forgave him as she went back with him.

Once they were back he threw his arms round Mary and kissed her in a way that was quite simply pitiful. Laying her across the bed, he pleaded with her: "My darling. Please, please forgive me, I beg you, but I've got to leave you for a while. I'll be back soon. When I do I'll tell you why and fill you in on the details. In a word, you must understand me. I love you so much, but I'm busy. Later on I may be able to fix things so that I'm a bit less busy, but at the moment it's just not on. So, you have a sleep. I'll sort your things out when I get back. Go on, shut your eyes, and don't be angry with me. I'm off."

Mary, by now thoroughly confused, lay on the bed, looking at him abstractedly.

He turned and went out of the room. His rapid footsteps on the stairs was all that could be heard.

As soon as he left Mary he forgot about her. As he rushed along the streets he thought of the people who were waiting for him. They must surely be even more anxious than he was.

3

The beautiful and lively young woman was left alone in the wide bed. She had brought a tender heart and powerful emotions with her from that place so far away. She was ready to give generously many good things and much tenderness to that man, provided only that he courted her properly. It really was because she needed this kind of attention and controlled roughness that she had faced the rigours of the long sea voyage. But what had she got for it? She was being neglected. He'd dumped her all by herself to go off somewhere else. What could be more important than meeting the woman he loved again after so long a separation? She lay on the bed for a long time, feeling thoroughly put out. Under the yellow light of the sixteen-watt bulb reflected from the ceiling she longed for Wangwei, feeling angry at the same time. What he had done had somehow hurt her pride. She wished that she could take her things and go off by herself to a hotel just to show him. But she loved him too much. She had lost much of her former ruthlessness, and was willing to put herself out a little in order to forgive him. Perhaps he really did have something even more urgent to do. Perhaps he'd be back that very moment. She pulled herself together and got up to sort out her things. As her face felt uncomfortable she wanted a wash. Even more urgent was a change of clothes. It would be a great mistake to wear that coat in here, getting it rubbed against everything. She opened all sorts of pretty little things in red and green that she picked through and stood one by one on his table. Only then did she notice that the table was completely empty. She brought out some superior packages containing fine presents she had brought for him — a handsome tie, two embroidered silk handkerchiefs, some cuff links and other things.

As she held them in her hands her feelings softened again. She imagined how happy he would surely be when he saw them in a few moments. He'd be bound to find her more adorable than ever. She piled the presents with loving care in a corner of the table. Finally she took a lightly wadded cheongsam out of the bottom of the case, a slightly worn one in black silk. As she stood in front of the mirror she took off her coat, catching sight of her beautiful body in the dim light. Under its heavy canopy of thick, black hair her face with its touch of pink looked both proud and affecting, delicately set off as it was by the high, bright green collar of the thin dress she was wearing. As she slowly unbuttoned it the pink scalloped edge of a slip came into view. Casting an admiring and flirtatious gaze over her half-naked flesh she dwelt with special appreciation on her white neck and arms before she finally brought herself to cover them with the quilted dress. The hem of the dress came right down to her heels, making her seem taller than ever. She was very beautiful and very attractive. Whatever colours or styles she wore only made her lovelier than ever.

On opening the wardrobe she found it almost completely bare, with not a garment inside apart from a few pairs of socks flung into a corner. A few empty clothes-hangers hung there forlornly. They gave her an involuntary start. She wondered if Wangwei had a trunk somewhere else in which he kept his things. When she had hung her exquisite clothes up in the wardrobe she started to look for Wangwei's case. She found two under the bed. As the bookcases were filled with his books she thought that he had probably not yet unpacked his clothes, which would all still be stuffed into the cases. She remembered how little care he paid to his appearance. He was always ruining good clothes and usually dressed like a ragamuffin. Then she sorted out some more of her things, and although she put most of the essentials where they would be easily to hand the room was still a frightful mess. Her cases lay gaping open-mouthed on the floor, which was covered with torn wrapping paper. She felt much too tired to tidy it all up right away: it was not that there was very much to do, but she simply could not cope. Not wanting to see any more of this rubbish dump she angrily lay down on the bed to go to sleep.

Time had passed quickly: it was eleven already. But because she had been so busy finding all the things she loved and quietly admiring herself she had not noticed how late it was. When she had lain down exhausted it had been quite impossible to go straight to sleep, so she had started feeling lonely. She longed for Wangwei even more desperately than she had on the boat, and was unable to understand why he was still not yet back or how he could leave her so long in this cold, empty room. She could not help being suspicious of him: in the past all had been passion and sweetness between them.

She was young and beautiful, and of course had long drawn the attention of many a man. She was not ignorant of such matters: she understood them and happily accepted them. But she loved nobody other than herself. She knew that she depended entirely on the beauty that youth had given her. She wanted to stay on her throne for ever, and was not going to let anyone snatch it away from her. From all the novels she had read and films she had seen she knew that once a woman married her life was over. To be a docile housewife, then a good mother, loving her husband and her children, losing all other form of happiness for the so-called warmth of a family, then in an instant to find your hair turned white and your hopes all dashed when your husband was still healthy enough to be going out and fooling around. All you could do then was to cultivate benevolence and wait patiently to become a grandmother. What was the point in all that? It was something she could do without. She was very satisfied with her present freedom. Her family gave her a bit of money, and although she could not be very extravagant she had enough to get by on. She had plenty of friends she could treat like servants who obeyed her every whim. After she had been living this easy life for so long one might have thought that there had been some upsets along the way, but her heart had never been touched. It had all just made her face lovelier than ever and given her a kind of classic poise. She was now more attractive than ever.

She could have lived as she longed to and not lost the attraction she had for the opposite sex for some time yet, but she had been overcome by Wangwei's passion. She had changed all her ideas. She had always rated men's love very low, but everything that Wangwei did had shown that even though he was a man his love was not contemptible. His actions had touched her and made it very hard for her to hold out. Unwilling to succumb, she had fled back to Beiping. Beiping was full of people who loved her even more than he did, and she had always enjoyed her life there. Although she had amused herself and laughed with people this time as before she had been unable to get that noble, taciturn face out of her mind. This male quality had made a deep impression on her, and she had really longed to be with him again. What he had given her seemed to be not so much love as an unbounded new feeling of hope about life, about a real kind of life of which she had known nothing before. At that very moment, when she was missing him so much, he had come to Beiping in heroic pursuit of her like a true lover in a romance. This had been even more to her liking, which was why she had accepted and rewarded his bold declaration. That was how they had lived together for a while with romantic ardour.

She had been really happy and liked it very much, but as a woman used to her freedom she had gradually come to realize that she had made too great a sacrifice. She had been afraid. Afraid that her life might get too boring, afraid of becoming a mother, and afraid of losing her friends. It was simply not worth losing so many servants for the sake of one man. She loved Wangwei, and it was in order to keep her good impression of him that she had wanted a temporary separation. She was willing for them to be free lovers, even to be close friends for the rest of their lives, but not for them to be a married couple cuddling together like tame pigeons. That was why she had decided to leave again. She had gone home for a short while only to find the family more detestable than ever. This had strengthened her determination to leave Wangwei, which was why she had broken her promise and gone back to Beiping's freezing cold. She had wanted to live in the peaceful ancient capital for a couple of years until she graduated from university. At first she had enjoyed living there again, but before long she had started missing Wangwei. As the frequency of his letters had decreased her anxiety that this passionate man would give her up had grown. In the end she had decided to sacrifice everything and come to Shanghai. She really could not bear to be separated from him. Cursing herself for being such a fool she had remembered their life together in the past. That really had been living. All the rest was nothing. Thereupon she had set out, bringing all her ardour to fling into the arms of her lover, the passionate lover of her dreams whom she had loved and respected.

But now she felt thoroughly let down. His treatment of her had come as a complete shock. She was angry and miserable. She waited till midnight and then until one before she heard footsteps tiptoeing quickly up the stairs. Once she was sure they were Wangwei's she felt cross again, and without her realizing it a tear fell silently on the sleeve of her black quilted gown.

4

As Wangwei crept quietly in he thrust all his other problems and difficulties out of his mind. He prepared himself to put up with the tortures of her love, and to give her as much tenderness as he could. He knew that she would find it hard to forgive him for what he had done that evening as she had not yet learned about how his outlook on life had changed. He wanted her to know about it in due course so that she could give him sympathy and encouragement and share his views completely.

Tiptoeing silently to the bedside he bent down to look at Mary. She made no sound and seemed to be asleep. He sat down beside her, not wanting to disturb her. The room, like his mind, was too chaotic and overcrowded for him to sort out. For example, he wanted to carry on with his work, but he also wanted to live with Mary. He felt that he had neither the time nor the strength to cope with both. The best thing would be to talk it through with her, so that she would be happy too and they would always be able to work together. Apart from their love they could often talk about all sorts of important questions, such as international economic and political problems and how to win freedom for working people. When their views were different they could argue fiercely. Perhaps she would be right, and in the end they would make it up — they were lovers, after all. He bent down over Mary to look at her again. She was so lovely, with an aristocratic kind of beauty. Every part of her body showed that only a happy life was right for her, only the best food and the freshest air. All her movements were suitable only for high society. Then he thought that if she could get rid of those fine clothes and wear a coarse cotton overcoat it might set her beauty off even better. If she could become a little rougher it might well bring out another kind of loveliness in her that it would be hard to put into words. As he looked again at her she seemed to have changed. There was about her something of the stubborn strength he dreamed of, even a touch of masculinity, as well as all the beauty and charm she had always had. He wanted to kiss her but stopped himself in case it woke her up. Then he started thinking again. Many thoughts went through his mind, mostly dreams about her, dreams of a happiness that she would not yet be able to understand.

He did not know how much later it was when he lay down beside her. Although he was utterly exhausted his mind was completely clear. He saw how solid and bright his future life was going to be, and he was keeping control over his happiness just like a helmsman keeping hold of a rudder. But he was too tired and his head ached too badly for him to be able to go to sleep. As his thought raced on and on he kept smelling the scent on Mary's body. He wanted to recover his energy and feel savage desires for her.

He lay so close to her that she could hear the fierce pounding of his heart, and his quick breathing was tickling her. She had been awake all the time, but had been ignoring him as she was still angry with him. Now she could take no more, so she turned quietly on her side to get a little further away from him.

Thinking that she had been asleep all along he asked, "Are you awake, Mary? I've been waiting for you for ages."

He stretched his arm out to her.

She pushed him away, saying in a very cold and quiet voice, "I've been awake all the time."

Her tone of voice told him everything. He clung to her with pity, pleading with her: "Won't you let me explain to you, Mary? You must see that you've misunderstood me. Take pity on me. You've given me so much. I'd be grateful to you for the rest of my life just for coming all the way from Beiping to see me, even if we'd only been able to spend an hour together. So however much you make me suffer now, even if you go on being this cruel, it serves me right. But don't be unfair to me, Mary. It's not that I mind being at the receiving end, but that I can't bear the pain of seeing you being angry when you shouldn't be. I know that you're angry with me. You may even be suspicious of me. Will you let me explain? I really am. . . ."

"No, no more. I hate explanations. Explanations are meaningless nonsense. I'm not angry with you. You're free to arrange your time as you will. My only regret is that in my weakness I overestimated the value of love."

"I don't want us to ruin our lives, Mary. I don't want a quarrel on the first night of our happiness. I was wrong, but one day you'll forgive me. You don't know how much I love you." He stretched his hands out to hold her again.

She was still in a bad mood, but she did not want to say any more. She let him hold her.

After this he started using love to win her gradually round again. Patiently he kept saying things that would soften her heart, and when the moment was right he started misbehaving a little, which made her like him all the more. This was not play-acting, but because he knew that it was the way to make the woman he loved more affectionate to him. These techniques were essential and at the same time sincere. Mary did indeed soon forget her unhappiness of a few moments earlier as she pillowed her head on his wrist and said, "You were so late back. I was really desperate. Are you always so late home?"

He replied that often he was. Usually he had things to do when he was out, and even when he did get back early sometimes he still was not able to sleep. He told her that he was very lonely in the room by himself.

He leant over her and stroked her face and hair. Feeling that he was a lot thinner than he had been before, Mary put her hand on his cheeks and said, "You've lost a lot of weight, Wangwei."

"With you here I can gradually feed myself up again," he replied.

But she thought of how he was busier than ever and never had any time off.

The two of them had by now forgotten their exhaustion, and they now had a very great deal to say to each other, the sort of things that one might expect only children to say, ridiculous things, things whose significance only people in love could understand. Only when the eastern sky began to turn pale did they fall asleep in each other's arms, forcing themselves to lie there quietly so as to recover their strength.

Because they were so much in love he was still as ardent as ever, and she was even more tender. Thus it was that they had another short spell of happiness and harmony together.

5

Usually he got up rather early, a little after eight. After perfunctorily tidying his room he would read the papers, stocking his head with a great deal of news. He wanted to bring together all the information he could get on the world economy. He was also collecting reports on the progress of the Chinese revolution and signs of the ever-worsening collapse of the ruling classes in order to show whether or not the present political line was correct. He also had to go through many reactionary papers for their contradictory arguments and for the signs that they were spreading false rumours and deceiving their readers. He particularly liked the *North China Daily News* as its reports were much more reliable than those in all the big Chinese papers, came faster than the popular tabloids and had some even more exciting stories than they did, ones that could never be found in certain Chinese papers. The English papers printed those thrilling reports under big headlines, not hiding anything. Yet they made no secret of the fact that they discussed the Chinese revolution from an imperialist point of view. They were trying to wake the Chinese warlords up by telling them about the growth and the strength of that other force, which was certainly not just the bunch of bandits that some said it was. Of course, Wangwei disliked their line of argument: he was only looking for accurate and stirring news. Of course, he also had to read other kinds of paper for their speeches and reports, for their resolutions on international politics, on China, on construction and on the revolutionary line, as well as for their news on what was happening in the factories. Sometimes he had to write other things too, such as drafts of plans and work programmes. At times like that his head would be bursting with all the ideas and proposals that welled up in it, but he still had to take more in, do more careful thinking, and bring all his thoughts together in an orderly way to write them up. He was not much used to this kind of work: three months earlier he had still been an unhappy student. If it had been a matter of writing poetry or something of that sort he would have found no difficulty in dashing off a few moving, touching and brilliant lines.

When he had almost finished rushing through his daily tasks the beautiful woman woke up. She was very spoilt: as she lay with her hair spread over the pillows and saw that her man was not in front of her she started to make angry little noises. Realizing that it was time to stop work, Wangwei put down everything he was doing and went to her bedside. Two lotus-like white arms were stretched out on the green quilt. From the neck of her embroidered pink and white jacket part of her delicate breasts could be seen. The touch of pink that peacefully suffused her after her deep sleep outlined her brows, eyes, nose and lips more clearly than ever, and made her shadowy declivities even more eye-catching. He was bewitched by this lovely body. Sometimes he kissed her fiercely and sometimes he dared not kiss her at all, but just gazed at her with devotion and adoration. When he did this she would always say with charming pettishness, "You got up early on the sly again."

At this he started making his explanation, sometimes in words, and sometimes more with deeds than with words. He was as devoted to her as ever and adored her. Even if at times she was a little displeased with him for not spending as much time with her as before she still had to forgive him.

She wanted to stay a little longer in bed before getting up, so he got in with her. What a gentle pleasure it was. They did not worry about anything, but kissed endlessly to their hearts' content, and talked all sorts of nonsense. She was so adorably naive.

Because she had been in bed so long her head was

starting to ache slightly, so she indulged in a long, lazy stretch then climbed out from under the quilt. She wanted to get up. Her little white feet jumped up and down on the quilt, so he quickly got up to rush around finding her all the delicate little things she needed, such as her garters, her silk knickers, and all sorts of feminine things to which he could not put a name. She wanted to be washed, have her hair combed, and her clothes changed. He of course was most attentive in his attendance on her. She was very satisfied at having in him so gentle and also so happy a slave.

By the time they went out hand in hand to a little local restaurant for breakfast it was quite late. Sometimes they went to a Cantonese restaurant as she was so fond of Cantonese cooking. Sometimes it was to a little Western-style cafe as she thought such places were a little quieter. By now he was growing somewhat impatient, though he did not show it, as he looked at the clock on the restaurant wall. He would have to be going very soon as he had not much time left to spend with her, but the moment of parting from her every day was always a difficult one.

After breakfast they went back to their room again. He could not help rushing, and as she knew they were soon going to part his haste irritated her. For a long time she said nothing. All he could do was to set out a little later. It was a far from happy moment when he planted an apologetic kiss on her cold, cold face and hurried off to the place he went to every day.

He was always late these days, and he was more rushed than ever as he translated the various documents. A discussion of some other matters was going on at another table, but even though he wanted to take

part he did not have had the time to do so: all he
could do was to glance in that direction from time to
time. Short little Feng Fei, smiling happily, was looking at him and saying, "What's up? Something else
seems to be on your mind these days, and you're getting more and more tired."

He just gave an inattentive grunt. He had simply
not had the time to observe how Feng's rather flat face
had been glowing a little more brightly every day. Feng
Fei and the conductress were now very good friends.

As soon as he had rushed through that job he had
to hurry off elsewhere. It was not always to the same
place. Sometimes he had to go a long way for a meeting, which demanded a lot of his time, energy and
thought. Any number of problems that were gnawing
at people's minds were brought together there, and as
there was never unanimity arguments would go on
and on, so that the meeting would only end around
supper time. As it was too far away for him to get
back in time he was usually unable to eat with Mary.
In addition he was busy most evenings, and hard
though he tried to cut back on these commitments they
were all essential. The earliest he could get back was
by eleven, and even then he would be feeling uncom-
fortably guilty towards a number of people for getting
away that early.

Sometimes, when he happened to be free, he would
get back for supper. These were the happiest of times
for Mary, when she had him for the whole evening.
When it came to the pleasures of being in love she
was never satisfied for a single moment. She dragged
him along the streets to find little restaurants they had
not visited before, and occasionally to bigger ones as

well. After their meal they would wander along the shopping streets bright in the electric lighting that threw all sorts of strange shadows. It would still be too early for the late show at the cinema. She often dawdled in front of the shop windows where the finest merchandise was on display, pointing at something and saying with astonishment in her voice, "Oh, that one's lovely."

Wangwei, who was not in the least interested in such things, had to smile and humour her. Sometimes she felt so cross with him for fobbing her off that she would give him an even more irritated look and ask him, "What's wrong with it? Look! It's exquisite!"

The only answer Wangwei could find was, "Yes, it's terrific. The rich really know how to live it up. But the day will come when we'll confiscate the whole lot." He was really only joking, trying to cheer her up, but she lost her temper and replied perfectly seriously, "Trust you to think that. I don't really want any of those expensive luxuries."

With a curl of her lip she walked away from the glass showcases, making a great show of her contempt for them. This gave her a new kind of beauty, like a proud queen. He expressed his admiration for her while she slowly and unconcernedly broke out into innocent, child-like laughter.

When they had enough time she would insist on hurrying back to the big shops to buy fruit, where it was of course excellent but expensive. She never bothered herself with petty calculations as she unstintingly told Wangwei to pay. Wangwei had been very hard up recently and would often walk a long way before catching a third-class tram, but on occasions such as these it was usually her money that they spent. Even though he felt she was being rather too extravagant he did not like to say anything about it.   He was completely obedient to her.

After that they would walk to the very grand cinema, buy their tickets, climb an ornately decorated staircase and go to their seats through doors beside which stood beautiful usherettes.   At times like that she would be extremely happy, whether or not the film had started and whether or not she liked it. She had spent a great deal of money, and extravagance is one of the best ways of satisfying vanity. She was now sitting in a magnificent place of entertainment of the kind that can only be found in Shanghai. From time to time the fragrance of perfume would waft over from the foreign ladies sitting nearby. She was more beautiful than them and had no need for cheap cosmetics. Some people would be looking at her and Wangwei. Wangwei was handsome too, with a masculine beauty that showed his unshakable firmness and unassailable dignity. She loved that, but he was not at all well turned out. His clothes were a mess, and no matter how often she spoke to him about it he still would not smarten himself up.   He hadn't had a new suit for years, and now that he was so poor there was even less hope than ever of him getting one. She had wanted to give him a decent overcoat but he had refused. He did not really need one, and he had not the time to order it.

When the film started she was always satisfied, no matter what it was like. She did not go to the cinema to be moved by the plot: the stories in her imagination were even better. She had even less need of finding out about American thought and art. She knew about everything on the screen already, and said she could always read a book if she wanted ideas and art. She went to the cinema simply for pleasure. Of the dollar she spent to go to the pictures eighty cents was for the upholstered seats, the illuminated bronze balustrades, the velvet curtains and the soft music. Only peasants went to the cinema just to see the film. -

Wangwei had been a film fan once, and had often gone to the cinema when he was at a loose end. He had liked romantic plots, amazing tragicomedies, and beautiful half-naked bodies. But now he was too busy and was not interested in appreciating that sort of thing. Those pointless movies were now utterly boring to him, no matter how many millions or even tens of millions had been spent on them. Sometimes he even hated them for the way they drugged people and had such a bad influence on society. They really were not things for him or people like him to watch: they were only fit to while away the time of the wives and daughters of capitalists. But for the sake of Mary, who loved him, he often put up with them. When he remembered how often he left the poor girl alone at home it was making some kind of recompense when he put himself out in this way for her happiness.

After staying out till late they would finally get back home. Mary apparently still wanted more. But when she saw how dead tired Wangwei was she could only forget about such ideas. Wangwei was really much too exhausted. His eyes were red, his head ached, and all the bones in his body felt painful. When he got home he always went straight to sleep the moment his head touched the pillow. This was something Mary regretted.

6

That sort of life could be regarded as very happy, but as time went on it became impossible to sustain it. Wangwei was simply too exhausted. He never had enough sleep. Mary, on the other hand, was too bored. Loneliness irritated her. "I think the way we were before was best," she often used to say to him. "How can I bring you back to me so that you'll always be mine? I suppose it's just a woman's dream. Oh dear, Wangwei. The thought of my weaknesses, women's weaknesses, is enough to make me hate men."

Wangwei realized that they were not getting on well together. If Mary had been a countrywoman, or a woman factory worker, or a middle-school student he could have led her and she would have followed. But Mary came from a fairly wealthy family and had never known hardship. Her intelligence only made her arrogant, and her knowledge only strengthened her attitude to life, which was one of extreme hedonism. She was self-confident and did not yield to others. Sometimes she could be even more stubborn and obstinate. Wangwei could see the crisis facing them like the crisis of the world economy, but he loved Mary. In the first place for her flawless beauty, but also because she was really intelligent, capable and brave. Her shortcomings were that she came from too good an environment, that she was besotted by her beautiful illusions, and that she refused to come into contact with reality as it was too tiresome and too much trouble, and especially because it was — as she saw it — too ugly and too vulgar. She was already twenty, and what mattered most to her was preserving her youth. She did not want to let troubles take her youth from her. Wangwei understood all this very well. He was always looking for ways of saving her, but the methods he tried were all too clumsy. She would see through them and say with a mocking laugh:

"Another wasted effort, Wangwei. If I'd wanted to work for the revolution I'd have started ages ago. Believe me, I haven't lacked for chances to do so. The only thing is that it bores me. It's not that I don't believe in it. You don't need to do propaganda with me. As for you, I'm telling you, it's bound to cost you your life. You'll see. It's just not worth it. To be perfectly serious, if you survived you'd have a big role to play."

What she said was perfectly true. All that did rather bore her. She had never once talked to him about his work, and she did not read the literature he brought back with him. She was completely absorbed in herself, apart from reading articles in trashy newspapers about reigning student beauties, famous athletes, film stars and high-class prostitutes. Wangwei hated that side of her, and sometimes could not hold himself back from telling her off: "Mary, I think it's really disgusting of you to enjoy that sort of thing. You never used to be like this before."

Mary would always answer along such lines as: "If you were at home I wouldn't read them. But I'm so lonely I need something amusing to while away the time. Those books of yours are no fun at all."

"Then come out with me. Wouldn't that be fun in its way?"

She made a face at him and burst out laughing.

Repeated promptings finally had some effect on her. She really was very lonely. So one day Wangwei took her to an unimportant meeting.

She started dressing for it with great care after lunch. She reckoned that all the other people at the meeting would be very badly turned out and look even more pathetic than Wangwei. She had heard that they were all very poor. It was not that she was arrogant and wanted to dazzle them, but she wanted to astonish them with her beauty. She wanted to set the heads of all those revolutionaries in a whirl. She found her outrageous notions very pleasing, as she did the triumph she imagined.

Having failed to find a single flaw in repeated inspections of herself in the mirror she felt satisfied. She sat down to wait very anxiously until Wangwei came rushing back at three, breathless and panting, to fetch her. She wanted to take another look at herself in the mirror and win Wangwei's admiration for her skill in making herself look so good, but there was no time. When Wangwei saw that she was already dressed up he just said cheerfully, "Good. I was worried you might not be ready yet. Let's go. I'm late again."

Paying no attention to how beautifully dressed and made up she was, he rushed straight ahead.

They were indeed late. As the discussion was now on the methods by which a certain job should be done and on the right pace to choose, the latecomers were not given a warm welcome. People just exchanged some glances with them and carried on with the discussion. As Wangwei led Mary to take a seat at a corner of a table a voice said very quietly, "You so-and-so, Wangwei. You're always being late for meetings. If you go on like this we may have to punish you."

Nobody paid any attention to her. To her distress only a couple of them gave her even a cursory glance.

She looked at the people there. There were seven or eight of them. Two wore long serge scholars' gowns, and the rest were in Western clothes. They were all young apart from two who looked shrivelled-up, and they all had something in common: they were very excited and bursting with a life force that came out on their faces. She noticed this as that life force was something she did not have.

She had often been excited, but it had been a very different kind of excitement that made no contribution to life. It had been all debauchery, idleness, the pursuit and enjoyment of physical pleasures. Although there were occasions when this could be attractive and captivating, in a place like this it seemed colourless and ugly. As she became half aware of this she began to feel a pain she could not have put into words.

Wangwei seemed to have forgotten her completely at this moment. He seemed more serious than ever. He had more to say than anyone else, and he did so very concisely. He ignored her, not giving her so much as a glance. More than once she gave his elbow a little push to show how awkward she was feeling, but he did not notice. All he did was to move his elbow further away. Gradually she began to resent the way he was behaving.

The longer the meeting went on the more bored

she felt. She did not want to listen to what they were saying: it was nothing to do with her. She did not know why, but she was starting to hate those people. All she wanted to do was to leave, but she had no chance to speak to Wangwei. It was five o'clock, then six, and then it was getting dark. From the look of it the meeting was never going to stop, and she was feeling uncomfortable. If she could have expressed her bad temper she would have felt better. Finally she stood up decisively. Only then did Wangwei ask, "What do you want?"

"There's something else I have to do," she replied proudly. "I'll go first."

"Fine. I'll soon have finished." Wangwei stood up for a moment and passed her the crimson handbag she had forgotten.

Everyone was looking at her and watching her leave, but there was no admiration in their eyes.

With calculated arrogance she walked out as if she were an aristocrat. The meeting continued uninterrupted till it finished at half past seven. As Wangwei was picking up his hat to leave, Shuyin, who had chaired the meeting, asked, "Are you free this evening?"

Wangwei thought for a moment before answering, "Yes."

"Let's have a meal together." As he spoke Shuyin took a dollar out of his pocket and examined it.

Remembering Mary, Wangwei said that he had to go back.

"We haven't got time. It'll take you a good hour to get back to your place from here. Are you worried about that woman of yours waiting for you?"

As Wangwei hesitated Shuyin continued, "Was the

young lady who came this evening the woman you wanted to put up for membership of the association?"

"Yes. I think she'd be a very capable worker. I really hope she'll be willing."

Shuyin gave a slight frown and lowered his voice without realizing it as he added, "I think you're onto a loser, Wangwei. She's a woman with a closed mind."

Wangwei gave a hint of a nod. "I'm dreading that painful moment," he replied. "It's more than Mary could stand. I know that she's had to put up with far too much already."

So he decided to go home for supper. He waited for a long time, but she did not come back. It was agonizing. As he realized that this was what it was like for Mary, always having to wait for him, he felt more and more sorry for her. He prepared himself to show her a lot more warmth when she did come back.

7

It was not until midnight, when he was almost asleep with exhaustion, that Wangwei heard her high heels coming up the stairs. He got up to welcome her, feeling very uneasy. In the electric light he could see no sign of unhappiness in her face. "Aren't you asleep yet?" she asked cheerfully and brightly. "I'm sorry to have kept you waiting so long."

She stood in front of the wardrobe, examining her burning face.

"Where've you been, Mary?" Wangwei calmly asked.

"No need for you to know. It's nothing to do with you. Tell me, how often have I interrogated you?"

"But. . . ." Wangwei went over to her, wearing a pathetic expression. "Are you cross with me, Mary?"

"No." She laughed and planted a kiss on his face.

"But you must tell me, Mary."

All Mary did was to laugh happily, unable to stop herself from showing her triumph at the sight of the deep furrows of suffering in his face. Her heart was filled with a cruel desire for vengeance on him. She wanted to torture him and make him suffer for having treated her so coldly, which was more than a passionate young woman could stand.

She would never be able to forget that meeting. She regarded it as a time when she had ceased to exist, especially in Wangwei's heart. She had been sitting so close to him, so how had he been able to put her out of his mind for so long, not giving her so much as a glance? He'd known perfectly well that this was not the kind of life she was used to. And when she left he had not seen her out or even said a few words to her. There had been a touch of cruelty in treating so proud a woman as herself like that. She had almost burst into tears as she left the meeting. She hated Wangwei, she hated the rest of them, and she hated that so-called meeting. She had sat there for hours and heard a great deal, but not one word of it all had won her admiration. How could they pretend that sitting and talking all day like that was working for the revolution? She had been thoroughly let down. It wasn't that she was against the revolution or was unable to work patiently, but if she was going to do something it was not going to be to sit around like that.

Her opinions were, of course, founded on her vanity,

but this business had also made her lose some of her respect for Wangwei. As she did not respect his work her contempt was irrational and hostile. The time he spent away from her was now intolerable. In the past she had made allowances for him because she loved him. She had not interfered and had respected his intentions. Now that she understood what it was all about she was determined to grab him back. He ought to have no other life except her. If he resisted she was going to make him suffer; she was going to take her revenge for all her love for which he had never repaid her.

Her mind made up, the first thing she had done was to go out for a fling by herself to let him see what it was like as he waited anxiously at home for her for a change. So she had taken herself to a restaurant for a meal. She had been the only person by herself in a restaurant crowded with young people in couples or in groups. The many astonished stares that came her way made her feel very uncomfortable, and she kept missing Wangwei. But before long a surprised and happy voice had called to her from a table opposite, "Mary, it's you!"

She had looked up and seen a woman of medium height in Western clothes hurry over towards her. Mary's heart had pounded with delight as she called back, "Hello, Molan."

They shook hands warmly and gazed at each other. It was quite a long time before Molan asked with astonishment, "Are you by yourself?"

Feeling rather ashamed, she had replied that the girl-friend she had come with had left to do something else, so that she was now on her own.

"Oh dear. You must be feeling terribly lonely. Come over and join us."

Mary wanted to refuse, but as Molan had already called over the waiter in white she had to go over to the table opposite with her. There were two men and another woman sitting there. Molan introduced them all to her, and she could see that they were all very stylish and fashionably dressed. Not one of them was as handsome as Wangwei, who did not have any of their vulgarity. As their eyes were all on her she pulled herself together and perked up. With a mixture of flattery and genuine admiration Molan said, "We haven't seen each other for almost a year. How do you do it, Mary? You're lovelier than ever?"

Everyone gazed at the clothes she had chosen so carefully, at the look she had worked on for so many hours to win a gasp of admiration.

She and Molan had been good friends before, and meeting her again just when she was feeling lonely had cheered Mary up. She ate her supper in a very good mood.

Molan had wanted to go to see where she was staying, but Mary had not wanted to go back so soon. She had invited Molan to go to the cinema with her and Molan, who also enjoyed such treats, had of course agreed. Mary had deliberately chosen a cinema a long way from the flat so that she would be even later back and Wangwei would have to wait even longer.

Everything had gone as she had hoped. Wangwei had suffered terribly waiting for her. She did not have to give him any searching looks to know that she could feel satisfied with what she had done. Although later on she had told him where she had been, unable to hold out against his pressure, she never mentioned Molan. He felt very unhappy on her behalf and offered to take her out in future as it was too lonely by oneself and he felt sorry for her. Mary said very little, as if all this were a matter of indifference to her. She gave a few sleepy yawns, took off her gown, got into bed and went very peacefully to sleep.

The next day Wangwei was out of bed as usual before he had slept enough, but this time Mary woke up soon afterwards and was out of bed without a moment's delay. She did not lift a finger to help him as he struggled with tidying up and other chores. All her attention was devoted to the mirror as she made herself up.

"Why are you up so early today, Mary?" Wangwei asked more than once.

"Couldn't sleep," was her indifferent reply.

At half past ten, when she was dressed and ready, she asked, "Shall we go out for our meal a little earlier today?"

"Why not? Let's go." He was feeling a little unhappy as she had interrupted this morning's tasks.

The two of them said very little to each other when they went to eat. It was as if there was nothing that needed to be said. On the way back Mary gave him a sweet smile and said, "There's no need for us to go back to the flat together. You can go to your job, or do whatever else you have to do. I think I'll go and visit a friend I haven't seen for ages."

Giving him a look to say goodbye she hurried off in the opposite direction from the flat. Wangwei hurried after her to ask her where she was going. She replied firmly and angrily, "Leave me alone."

Wangwei wanted to ask her more and say other things to her, but she jumped straight into a rickshaw. He could only gaze disconsolately at her back as she disappeared, then listlessly turn and go back to the flat. It was a complete mess, with everything all over the place. Her discarded clothes and stockings were everywhere. The face bowl was full of dirty water on which floated cream, powder and grease. He had intended to use this spare moment to do a little more work, but he would not get Mary out of his mind. He did not hate her but was only sorry for her. The reason why she had left him like that was because she was still angry with him: of that he was sure. Despite her acting so cold she was really very unhappy. He lay on the bed that was still full of her scent thinking about everything to do with her, about her future, about her intelligence, about how he had never wanted them to split up. He wanted them to make the same journey, hand in hand, and hoped that Mary would be able to change with the times. She would not go on drifting like that. He really had to live with her.

8

From then on Mary did not spend much time at home. She went out to see Molan and many other women friends she had not seen for ages. She was not particularly lonely without him, but she still loved him and always felt a touch of pain. Wangwei was miserable too. He could see ahead more clearly than she could. If Mary left him one day and flew away, he thought, it would of course be hard for him to bear, but it would hurt her much more. He was very busy and would make himself busier. His faith would endure and would not depend on whether a woman left him or not. Although he would have a very tough time he would be able to use another source of strength, his ideals, to overcome what remained of love's weaknesses. But Mary was only a woman fond of dreams and pleasures, spoilt by her environment and too weak to save herself. Her suffering might even destroy her. He thought about her very thoroughly and for her own sake he must try to win her round. But he had too few chances to do so. Mary came back very late every evening, sometimes after he had gone to bed. She often got up even earlier than he did, and was very cold: whenever he tried to say a few affectionate words she would find ways of stopping him. Despite the kindness of his intentions he was too busy to think about such matters all day. One evening, when he had just folded back the covers before going to bed, Mary came back, her face flushed from having drunk a little too much.

"Just look at yourself in the mirror, Mary," he said involuntarily. "You're so lovely."

In the past such praise would have delighted her and won an even more bewitching smile. But today she only snapped, "Don't talk such rubbish."

She went to sleep looking very selfish, her mouth firmly shut. Although he was sleeping beside her Wang-wei felt no breath of tenderness from her. At the thought of their past warmth and love he could not help sighing.

"What are you sighing for? You're keeping me awake," said Mary.

"I was thinking about the way we were before. . . ."

"That's all in the past. It's not worth thinking about."

"It was a lovely time. I hate to say it, Mary, but you've hurt me a lot."

After this Mary flared up. With terrifying violence she yelled at the top of her voice:

"I've hurt you? Nonsense! It's you who've been hurting me. What pain are you feeling? Every day you've got your so-called work and all your comrades. You've got hope and an aim in life. When you come back in the evening you can rest and you've got a woman you can kiss without so much as a by-your-leave. What about me? I've got nothing. I just drift around all day. All I've got is masses of boredom, loneliness, and the regrets of lost love. But I put up with it. I stay with you as an amusement for you when you're tired. I've never breathed a word of complaint. And now it's you who's sighing and blaming me. . . ."

Anger choked off the rest of what she had been going to say. She was caught in a terrifying spasm.

Wangwei had wanted to let fly at the nonsense she had been talking, but seeing the lunatic way the woman was behaving he held himself back and said, "Don't be like that. Don't be like that."

Mary made no sound for a long time as she lay there with her head buried in the quilt. Later on Wangwei heard very quiet sobs coming from her quilt. He could not help turning her towards him, although he was worried she might reject him. Though Mary ignored him, she did nothing either. Her tears had overwhelmed her. He held her gently in his arms and said softly, "It's my fault, I know. Please forgive me, Mary. Don't cry, I beg you. It'll ruin those eyes I adore."

She paid no attention, just continuing to sob.

There was nothing he could do except wait patiently blaming himself for faults he did not understand and making absurd vows. As she would not stop crying, he ended up feeling very miserable. Ever since they first met they had got on very well together. Now they were beginning to split up and Mary was so unhappy. As he thought over the way things had gone he felt that nothing could be done to save the situation. Perhaps they would never be able to get on well together again; perhaps Mary might leave him now. He could not hold back his unhappy tears, the first tears he had shed for many years.

As his tears fell on Mary's face they had a heavy impact on her heart and softened it. She raised her hand to stroke his face, which was wet, and his thin cheeks, which made her unhappier than ever. She started sobbing aloud.

He held her very close and pressed his wet face against her even wetter one.

"I love you, Mary."

Mary let him kiss her and returned his embrace. After a while she said, "I'll always love you, Wang-wei."

With that the barriers that had been keeping them apart disappeared. Mary's hatred vanished as she lay in his arms, whispering her troubles to him. He then told her of his hopes. Mary felt once more that he loved her, which made her happy. He felt more cheerful too as he had a chance to tell her what was on his mind. As she trusted and believed him he had the impression that his dreams were not far from being realized. He felt that women were all like that. It was much easier to move her through love than to convince her through reason. This was not something he wanted in a woman: quite the contrary. But that was the way Mary was, and he was very happy with the fact, because it proved that he loved her.

The two of them talked all night, holding each other close with the tenderness that follows grief, then slept through the morning.

9

That afternoon he arranged to come back early. Mary was so tired that she was still in bed. Her eyelids were slightly puffy, and her face shone with a pallor that made her look a little drawn and weak but even more adorable. He took her hand, which had no strength in it at all.

"Why are you back now?" she asked.

"I'm slacking, of course," he said with a grin.

She was very happy, but she also said, "Don't do it again. I really don't want you to."

Wangwei came back early for many days, and did not go out at night either. He told people that he was a little under the weather, and as he had been looking so much more haggard in the last couple of months this was believed. The way he had worked himself into the ground before was also proof that he was not just making up an excuse. He really did need a short rest. But he never felt comfortable spending all his time at home alone with a woman.

Mary did not go rushing about any longer, but waited in for him. When he was out she did a little tidying up for him. She wanted to move to somewhere a little better and fix them up with some decent furniture. Wangwei agreed, not wanting her to have to live his own spartan life. Now that it was getting warmer she wanted some lighter, spring clothes. She enjoyed going out when she was reasonably well dressed, and it was very miserable if you couldn't go out in spring. Besides, she wanted to read some novels. The ones Wangwei bought her were all Soviet ones. His aim was to influence her through them in the hope that her tastes and ideas could gradually be changed. She understood why Wangwei went to all this trouble, but she only read them for entertainment, remarking that the plots were very fresh. Wangwei wanted to discuss other matters, but she only commented on the beauty of the style. Wangwei had to give up and revert to his old line of waiting patiently.

Thus it was that they had another spell of peace. But by now it was April, and as Wangwei had some connections with the General Labour Union he became busier, which left him with less free time than ever. Often he only came back to sleep. At first Mary had put up with this, but after a few days she became a little restive. She urged him to take her out, but he refused; and when she tried to make him spend a little more time at home he showed his irritation. He shook his head when she asked him about moving. Sometimes she tried to give him a scare:

"If you're never going to be in you'll come back one day and find me gone, Wangwei. Do you think I'm prepared to be a dutiful wife? Do you imagine that you can love woman without spending a bit of time with

her? What about it, Wangwei? I insist that you spend
sometime at home now. If you don't. . . ."

Wangwei shook his head helplessly. "Why do you
have to think along those lines?" He had to say. "I wish
you could be rational, Mary. Think it over. I really can't
wait another minute now: I've got to go this moment.
You ought to understand me and make allowances, not
carry on this way. If you want me to find you some
work that'll suit you you've only to say the word. We
need workers badly at the moment."

Mary collapsed on the bed in a fury, and Wangwei
seized the opportunity to make his escape, which made
her more miserable than ever. There could be no two
ways about it: Wangwei took his work much too
seriously. Love meant nothing to him. How could she
go on living with a man who did not love her?

She remembered what Wangwei had said: "If you
want me to find you some work that'll suit you you've
only to say the word." Hunh! What work would suit
her? She recalled the utter boredom of that meeting.
She couldn't possibly join that organization: she knew
herself too well to do that. It offered her no glory and
admiration, only idiotic boredom that was of no possible interest to her. It was true that she was not rational
and was ruled by her emotions. She did not deny that
this was the way she had always been. As he was
making no emotional impact on her there was no point
in forcing herself to change into what Wangwei wanted
her to be. Anyhow, she believed, no matter what she
did, even leaving him, would have no effect on him.
The facts showed that he had no need of her.

Unhappiness tormented her once more. She felt as
if she had somehow grown a lot older. This could not

be allowed to drag on and on, especially as she could see that he was not suffering. She no longer talked to him very much as she knew that there was no point. He said very little to her. He was very short of time, and whenever he mentioned anything about his work he could sense her lack of interest. The room was now filled with an air of misery, an atmosphere that enveloped her alone as he was so rarely at home. Although he was often elated she reacted very strongly against his excitement. Mary saw clearly where they were at odds, but could find no way of repairing the damage. If she could not obliterate her own self to turn herself into someone with a head like his she had to work out how to bring him back to her as he had been in the past. But could she? Her lack of confidence in her ability to do so made her feel more wretched than ever. He had not been like this before: he had changed completely in the short time she had been away from him. He was so ruthless now. She had no idea what could have given him the strength to be like that. It terrified her. She could not make that change with him. Her circumstances and her character were too different.

10

Time dragged on and on and the suffering grew worse. When Mary could endure no more she had no choice but to take the final step, a step forced on her by despair. One evening Wangwei found the room a little different when he came back. It never occurred to him that Mary really had gone until he went to bed and found it stripped. All that was left was his dirty old cotton-wool quilt. Mary's soft silk quilt had gone. Only then did he start to wonder what was up. When he opened the wardrobe he found all her dazzling clothes gone. All that was left was an untidy heap of clothes-hangers and his old overcoat. Her cases had gone too, and all her superior cosmetics had vanished from the drawers. Only then did he realize that the day he had most been dreading had finally arrived. As he gazed abstractedly around the empty room he did not know what to do. Shanghai was too big for him to go searching for her. Besides, how was he to cope with her even if he could find her and bring her back? Could he spend all his time with her?

"It was too soon," he kept saying, "it was too soon." He thought about how they had met, about the sweetness of their life together, about their separation and her return to Shanghai. He was unhappy himself, and even unhappier for her. He had destroyed her. If he had not loved and pursued her she would still be an innocent young girl living a happy and trouble-free life. As it was he had not only failed to convert her, but had given her very many sad memories. She would never be happy again unless she found another purer and more passionate love. Only love could save her, only a supreme love, not like his. He knew that he had been too cruel to her. He felt infinitely apologetic towards her, but he could not comfort her and would never be able to.

He lay on the bed feeling utterly despondent as he silently muttered the beloved name: "Mary, Mary. . . ."

The next morning he was still lying fully dressed on

the bed, utterly exhausted. His eyes were wide open but he could not bring himself to get up. When he heard the landlady knocking at the door he shouted, "Come in!" The white-haired old lady came in, her kindly red cheeks bearing as always the touch of a smile.

"I'm ever so sorry, sir, but I forgot all about it. When the young lady left yesterday she gave me a letter to give you when you came home. I waited a long time, but you were too late back." She brought a letter out from her clothes.

He snatched it from her.

"She told me that she'd had a telegram from home. Someone's ill. The young lady said that it's all written down here, and that you'd understand when you'd read it. The young lady gave me two dollars. I'm ever so grateful. She's ever so nice."

He tore the letter open. As the old lady was still standing there he had to say. "That's right. There are some problems at home. That'll be all."

Only then did the old lady slowly leave the room. The letter was straightforward:

Dear Wangwei,

I'm leaving. I know that this won't come as a surprise to you, but I ought to tell you. I'm going to stay with a friend while I wait for your reply. If you still love me I hope that your reply will satisfy me. If it doesn't we won't be meeting again. You ought to know the only reasons that have forced me to leave are that your love is untrue and I can't take your work. If you can't provide me with a full and satisfactory explanation and plan for putting things right there's no need to reply because no other reply will solve anything. You ought to understand me by now and realize what it is that has driven us apart. In other words, to put it bluntly, if Wangwei isn't Mary's, Mary would rather suffer by herself.

Mary

P.S. Write to me at Post Box 1782 at the General Post Office.

When Wangwei had read this he said not a word. He could not deny that this woman still had a powerful allure for him, and he remembered how his troubles disappeared when he lay in her arms.

That afternoon he made time to go to the General Post Office, but they maintained complete secrecy about box numbers, so he failed to find out any more information about her. That evening he still wanted to reply to her letter, whether or not his reply would satisfy her. If she came back he would be very grateful to her, and if she did not he would of course be very miserable. But he was not going to accept the responsibility for their separation: it was none of his fault. Rubbing his tired eyes and looking at Mary's letter he wrote on a blank sheet of paper:

Mary! You can imagine what a cruel time this is for me. This room, full of so many memories you've left me, is as desolate as a tomb now. I'm propping up my head, which is aching so much I'm almost fainting, and keeping my eyes open although they're hurting badly, to try and do this painful job: writing this letter as you've ordered me. There's no need for me to go into long explanations. One day Mary will see whether or not her Wangwei loyally fulfilled his duty in love. Mary ought to realize that the man she loves has never deceived her in the slightest. I'm convinced that this is no exaggeration and that Mary can understand this much: it is circumstances that have driven Mary away. The fact that she is fed up with Wangwei's conduct shows that he can no longer please her. This is far from what you had hoped for and has hurt you very badly. But this was of course not what I wanted to happen, and I can't take all the blame for it. Besides, I've suffered a lot too, and I probably started suffering before you. I tried to avert this terrible day, and you are clever enough to have understood long ago how serious I was about this. But this was all an illusion on my part. Your old attitude to life couldn't be changed in the least: your character is too proud. But I don't want to say any more about that. Now that the split between us has widened to a gulf you have to break away from me. I can't bring myself to say a word of complaint about your cruelty to Wangwei who has done you no wrong at all. This is because I know that Mary is in a state of even more hopeless grief than I am, as I can't give her a very satisfactory answer to the last hopes she had of me. Yes, I could say that if you came back I'd give everything else up and spend all my time with you, free from our troubles. But the fact is that I refuse to deceive you — as you know, I've never lied to you — and even if I could get out of my present work my beliefs can never change. From Mary's point of view Wangwei will probably never be a man worth loving.

In short, I don't want to say too much. I leave everything to your perceptive judgement. I can't very well be like a child howling for his Mary. Everything now depends on you. The final decision is yours.

With many apologies,
Wangwei

He waited anxiously for many days after the letter had been sent without getting any reply. The enquiries he made everywhere yielded nothing. Evidently his reply had made Mary decide finally that even more suffering was preferable to coming back. They were now cut off from each other, and neither could find a way of making this tragic story come right.

II

Life went back to the way it had been before Mary came. He was busy, busier than ever, but even though Mary's image faded and at times completely disappeared when he was busy, he missed her desperately when he lay alone in his bed. He worried about her, because he could not imagine how she would be living. He knew what a miserable state she was in. He had made enquiries everywhere in the hope of getting some comforting news about her, but with no success. Everything to do with her had disappeared with her. All he had left was a worried heart tied to the vanished woman.

One day towards the end of January, at about the beginning of the third week after Mary's departure, he was sent to make a speech at a very busy spot. When he arrived he saw that the street was full of their people. The people on the pavements, in the shop doorways, on the platforms at the tram stops and parading to and fro were all students and workers. In this solemn atmosphere the tall Indian policemen felt tense, walking to and fro with affected unconcern. As it was not yet the right time he was still strolling slowly along the pavement, assessing the situation. He felt a touch of excitement that he could not repress. It was as if he could already see the mountainous waves that were soon to come crashing down, and the volcano that was to erupt and burn the city to ashes. It was entirely possible and was indeed on the very point of happening: all those people were ready and waiting, and he was going to start the storm. There were some people he knew there whose hearts were also starting to burn. Calm could not cover their excitement. Their faces were all flushed with the pleasure of anticipation.

Just then a couple rushed past him. When he looked up he saw that one of them was their secretary, Feng Fei, full of excitement, his round face wreathed in smiles. With his left hand he was holding the hand of a spirited, healthy woman, his tram conductress. As soon as he noticed Wangwei he rushed up to him, smiling, as if he had a lot that he wanted to say to him. Wangwei could only give Feng a look and a slight nod before moving on. Feng Fei's smiling face was not an ordinary one: it stayed in Wangwei's mind. At the same time the image of Mary sprang back into his mind. So the dreams that had once been his were coming true for Feng. That woman was just what a revolutionary woman should be. But the time was soon coming: he would have to stop thinking about that.

He went to the outside of a public building where the crowds were even denser and there were a lot of people he knew well. They were all waiting for the first signal. Time dragged by, a minute at a time. At nine o'clock sharp there was an enormous eruption of firecrackers on the other side of the road, followed by the thunder of slogans being roared in response. An astonishingly loud shout of "In we go! Get the place for the meeting! Charge!" rang in his ears.

He pushed hard into the place and was carried along by an enormous force as they thrust their way in. The large platform was at once full of heads. A raucous babel filled the whole space. As he and a couple of other people shoved their way forward to the platform the loud voice rang out again:

"Quiet! The meeting is open! Where's the presidium!"

Silence fell at once. He had made his way to the side of the platform now, where he heard someone saying, "Come here, Comrade Wangwei."

He sprang on the platform and took his place in the chair. Another wave of cheers, and applause welled up. Shouting and gesticulating, he gradually quietened the audience down again. Calmly and solemnly he began to speak:

"We're here today for a meeting. First I want to explain what the meeting signifies and what it has to do. This is. . . ."

Two pistol shots rang out at the entrance to the hall and a crowd of police came charging in, so that the ranks of the masses began to waver and panic. With shouts of "Get them!" some excited and trembling voices echoed through the air. Others dispersed, running away from truncheons and bullets. As he watched this dramatic development Wangwei longed to be able to calm things down, but as more and more police poured in the audience was thrown into growing turmoil.

"Things are looking bad," a voice beside him whispered. "Let's move into the crowd." He jumped down with the other man, but just then a huge hand stretched out from the crowd and seized him by the shoulder. A giant of a man pushed against him and said:

"I've been on your tail for ages, you bastard. You're not getting away now. If you want to make trouble, come and make it at the station."

His arm was being twisted in an agonizing lock. At the sight of the sinister face he realized that there was nothing he needed to say to it.

"We must get ready to hold the — demonstration straight away," he went on shouting towards the crowd. "Down with imperialism!"

A big fist landed in his face, choking him, and he was dragged along the road. Many of the masses were scattering too. He could see the high emotion on their faces as they gave him looks of comfort and encouragement. He also heard some ragged slogans. Elsewhere the masses were battling hard with the police. He was forced to a Black Maria and flung inside. It was already full of prisoners. Looking out through the wire grille he caught sight of a beautiful and elegant woman at the entrance of a department store. It was Mary. She was as eye-catching as ever, and as graceful as if she were the queen of some faraway country. Her air was still one of happiness without frivolity. It was evident that she had just been doing some shopping as she was carrying many packages. And, yes, a handsome young man had his arm round her. As he gazed in alarm he said to himself:

"Fine. She's found happiness. So that's the kind of person she is after all. I don't need to worry about her any more. That's fine, Mary."

There was chaos inside the Black Maria as two more prisoners were flung inside, almost crushing him. A lot of angry voices could be heard saying, "If we're going, let's go, dammit. What are we waiting for?"

At once the wagon started to move and they were all thrown to the ground. They picked themselves up at once and shouted in unison:

"Down with. . . ."

". . . . . ."

1930

From Dusk to Dawn

"AN alley, lonely, a crescent moon high in the sky, stars twinkling, tram wheels grating along the lines, a child, an adored back, the two of them walking along, father and mother.... Rubbish! This is a load of nonsense."

She, a woman, had thought a lot and crossed out a lot but did not know how to get it right. She was now walking along the pavement, alone, towards what passed for home.

"This was the day my brother died all those years ago. I saw a lot of graves with paper money on them from the train. I've no idea where they buried him. Mum must be feeling very miserable right now. No, Little Ping can take her mind off the past. But . . . but why do I have to keep thinking about all that?"

After crossing the road she turned into an even quieter street planted with trees on either side. The street lights threw the shadows of the sparse new leaves at her feet. She could hear her own heels echoing on the concrete.

"Mm. Mum's letter. All that stuff the old lady wrote about happiness and joy. I want you to know that you scare me.... Never mind. At least Little Ping has a mother. How could you say that he isn't happy?"

Some people were hurrying towards her. She stepped aside and continued her indignant line of thought:

"You'll see what I'm going to do. I'm not scared of you."

A violin was being played very softly beside the road. It was the song of an utterly grief-stricken life. She stopped for a moment to listen before hurrying away.

"I won't, I can't listen to that."

She hurried straight to the alley where she was living. The smell of oil came from many kitchens. All the sitting-room lights in their red silk lampshades had been turned on, and some pianos were being played. She went up to a house smelling of opium smoke, knocked hard on the back door and shouted:

"I'm the woman who lives upstairs. Please open up."

As always, she had to wait for an age before the sallow-faced maid tiptoed to the door and opened it. Once inside she covered her nose and started going upstairs.

"Someone came for you." The maid stood at the foot of the stairs. Her hair was very long.

"Oh. Did they say anything?"

"No." The dirty face looked really pathetic.

"What's that to do with me?" She carried on up the stairs.

The room was completely empty and the light seemed to hurt her eyes. She threw herself on a chair. Her head was aching as if something were being jabbed into it. She looked listlessly around the room, but all she could see was a face with tears in its eyes: Adian, still laughing aloud. In that innocent childishness she could see that there was also a wildness. Poor girl. What a miserable childhood she'd had, so lonely, so unforgettably lonely.

She was dropping with exhaustion and her head was

still aching, so she shut her eyes in the hope of getting a little rest. But the sea still stretched out in front of her, and carefree gulls roaming proudly across the vast sky. She was exhausted after her outing. She had kept Yang company but what good had it done her?

" 'You and I should have been extinguished with the stars.' That was how a line in one of his poems went." But what ought I to be saying now?

"What? What ought I to be saying? I shouldn't be saying anything. I ought to understand that.

"What have the sea and the prairie got to do with me? I roam around all day, but nothing moves me.

"Why not? I shouldn't say that. I'm like everyone else, not different at all."

Yes, she had been moved. She remembered how when she got into the tram in the North Sichuan Road after coming back from Wusong she had seen the back of a man in a lined beige coat, a very familiar back. "Hey, Ping," she had almost cried out in delight, but then she had seemed to remember something. All she had done was to lean her head in sorrow against the tram window and hold back her tears. But she still turned to look, to search among those young people, half hoping that his familiar face would surface in the crowd. But it was impossible. The tram took her straight to the Nanjing Road where she had met Mrs F. This was how what had caused her most pain had begun.

With people crowding behind them she and Yang had gone into the Wing On Department Store. Many powdered faces flashed in front of her, and a record of a film star singing was playing on a gramophone. She had walked aimlessly upstairs, then down again. Without meaning to they had gone into the department selling

Western-style baby clothes. She had found herself
lingering there till she found just the thing she wanted,
a one-piece romper suit in beige and blue. There was
another suit beside it, a smaller one. This would fit even
better. She gazed and gazed at it, then counted the
money in her handbag. One dollar eighty. Not enough.
Nowhere near enough. She had felt thoroughly miserable, and remembered the latest letter from home saying
how sweet the baby was and how everyone adored him,
but they hoped his mother and father could see their
way to sending some money back so that he could be a
bit better fed and clothed. That would save the people looking after him from feeling so sad on his account.
And the milk powder had almost run out. . . . But the
romper suit had been in such lovely bright colours that
she could not tear herself away. Then she had seen some
pink silk girls' clothes and wanted to look at them. Just
then Yang had given her a hard push, making her look
up in surprise. Yang had given her a glance to make
her notice that a beautiful young married woman was
standing beside her and fingering a patterned baby's
blouse. As she looked at the woman's black cat-fur coat,
long hair and exquisite, lightly made-up face she had felt
a touch of giddiness and not known what to do. But
it had been nothing serious. She had lightly brushed
against Mrs F's arm, causing a slight astonishment to
appear on the other's face. Mrs F had spoken in her
usual very quiet way:

"Oh. . . . I haven't seen you for ages." Her voice
revealed deep feeling.

She had not known how to reply.

"Are you all well? Still living at the same place?"

She felt that the conversation was well-nigh pointless, but she did not want to go straight away.

"We haven't moved. I hear you've sent the baby home. . . ." Mrs F had continued, as quietly as before.

"Er . . . yes, that's right. . . . Are you buying clothes?"

"No, powdered milk." Mrs F had raised a large tin of milk powder that she had just bought.

Powdered milk. The letter from home had said that the milk powder was running out. . . . Another dizzy spell had moved across her eyes as a sudden wish seized her. "Come and see me, and bring the baby with you," she had said in a trembling voice.

"Yes. Are you by yourself now? Where are you living?"

She had hesitated for a while before slowly coming out with her address. She hoped Mrs F would be able to remember it.

"Goodbye then." She had left, turning her head back a little later to see that Mrs F had also left the counter. She had not bought the blouse.

"Poor thing," Yang had said with feeling. "Why did a young lady like her have to marry a — ist?"

"They love each other, and their love keeps them going." She had still been feeling a little dizzy, and her feet were not touching the ground.

"It all seems very contradictory to me." Yang was full of contradictions herself.

On Yang's instructions she had sat in a rickshaw, unable to hold her tears back any longer. What was the good of it? Nobody would know. Not even Mrs F would realize that she could make someone as tough as herself cry. She had remembered the past, a terrifying night in the past when the wind had howled and the fine rain had blown into her face as she had rushed all over the place, distraught. First she had gone to three familiar places and drawn a blank at each of them before finally going to Mr F's home. When she had seen the red-shaded light burning in their second-floor window she had been almost happy for a moment and had pounded at the door. But there had been no sound. She had run round to the back door, still without getting any response. In indescribable anxiety she had stood in the road shouting, "Mr F! Mr F!" Perhaps the road was too noisy: the upstairs window never opened once for her. A passer-by had knocked again at the door for her while she went on shouting from the roadside. The light had suddenly gone out. "They've gone to bed," she had said to herself in disappointment. She could imagine the three of them all asleep, all cuddled together. When she looked at the window again and saw it shutting in their sweet happiness she did not want to shout any more. She had just looked at it and wept, thinking of her new-born baby and the man who had been flung into some dark hole, she knew not where. She had cried for a long time till her hair was wet with her tears and the rain before hurrying home through the storm. That night had settled her destiny. She would never be able to see the man she loved again. Everything had gone, all that life of undisturbed sweetness, all the progress and hope that the two of them had shared. Had it all gone? Those unforgettable dreams?

She had not sobbed aloud in the rickshaw. Another force had been weighing down on her.

That night Mrs F's face, which had not lost its youth, appeared to her again. Putting up with her half-felt pain she had thought:

"They're still the same. I've seen them, I've seen their happiness. They're living the way we used to live, the life of our ideals. But their child must be older by now, old enough to be fun, old enough to have nice clothes. But I didn't see her buying that little blouse. Of course, they probably don't have enough money to spare...."

She had then remembered something that had happened not long before. Once when changing Little Ping's nappy she had noticed that his quilt was a little too short and said cheerfully while patting his little bottom, "Don't be such a trouble-maker, you little devil. You ought to show your parents a bit more consideration. Don't you realize you're growing too fast?" Little Ping's father, who had been sprawled in a chair reading at the time, had joined in the joke and said, "That's why I chose the name Trouble-maker for him, and quite right too. Oh yes, F's baby's got very few clothes. They tell me her quilt's too small and too thin." By then she had wrapped the baby up again and picked him up to say, "Very well. If we're going to get another quilt made, let's have an extra one made too. Are the F's hard up too?" "Of course. F told me that all they're living on is those two bookcases of foreign books. But I don't know what they're going to live on in another month...."

That month had long since passed. What were the F's living on now? She found herself feeling concerned and anxious for them. Of course, in her eyes they were happy, in a way that grieved her by reminding her of everything. But the remark about not knowing what they were going to live on had gnawed at her and disturbed her.

"She must be feeling very unhappy because she couldn't buy that blouse. Of course, that's not what really matters in their life, but things like that always upset a mother. Perhaps she's telling F about it at this very moment, and they're imagining how it would look on their darling little girl. . . ."

Yes, they were happy. F was like the man she loved, and Mrs F was still young and beautiful. She hoped they would always be like that. Probably they would be lucky and never meet with disaster. But. . . . She had felt dizzy again and been enveloped in darkness.

"Oh dear, she. . . ." She saw that face with a touch of make-up again. "On dear, she's happy now, but perhaps she doesn't even realize it herself. How can I help admiring and loving her? She's the image of what I used to be. . . . I want to, I'm going to buy that blouse and give it to her."

The thought excited her. She sprang to her feet, seized her purse and went out. Only when she was in the street did she remember something and look at her watch. It was 9:15. Very well then. That was what she'd do. She got five dollars from a pawnbroker's and hurried towards the Avenue Joffre.

Some shops had shut already, but bright lights shone from others. She had been here very often before, and she had remembered exactly where she was going to buy what she wanted. She had taken quite a lot of interest in children's things before. She went into a shop in front of whose windows she had often lingered before: she and Little Ping's father had worked out when the baby would be needing some of those things. It would be in spring, when the baby was older, and they could take him out in a pushchair. But only now was she coming here, and coming here alone to buy a little girl's blouse. She saw many things she knew well by sight and had once admired, but she had put up with the pain of it by thinking, "I'll give it to her: I want to cheer her up."

The old foreign lady brought out a whole pile of blouses in a kindly way and looked at the happy young mother with a kind and understanding smile. She chose a pink silk blouse embroidered with a flower. It had been, thank goodness, reduced to only $ 6.20.

The trams still grated along, cars still endlessly hooted, and clean-shaven young foreigners wearing elegant ties still sauntered along, arm in arm with their girlfriends, stopping every now and then in front of a shop window to point at exquisitely displayed jewellery. There were flower-sellers too. And from a musical instrument shop rolled waves of intoxicating singing. Everything was the same, everything was the same as in the past; in the past she too had strolled there.

She went back to her room and looked at the baby's blouse again. It really was a lovely one. As she refolded it she thought happily, "I reckon this ought to cheer her up." She enclosed a letter with it, a very polite and mildly-stated one: she did not want anyone else to know what she was feeling.

When everything had been smoothly done she felt as if she had fulfilled a vow. She lay on the bed, but remembered herself again, her past and her present, her baby whose powdered milk was running out. For the first time since she had been living alone she let herself cry her heart out.

"Why am I crying? Forget about it all! Why didn't I cry my heart out when I could have done so in my beloved's arms? I ought to pull myself together now. . . .

"Why shouldn't I? I ought to have a good cry. I've held it all in for too long. I ought to indulge myself more, like I used to before. I'm going to turn everything upside down, smash everything. All I want is a moment's gratification. . . ."

Her head felt very heavy and her heart was hurting as if it had been wounded. She almost felt that this was the end of her.

What was the time? It was so still, so terrifyingly still. The light was too bright, but her face and her expression were too pale, too grief-stricken.

She did not know when she drifted off into a death-like sleep.

The sky was beginning to lighten, but the yellow light bulb was still on. She woke up as usual and sat up with a start. She never allowed herself to lie in bed once her eyes were open, afraid as she was that those pointless fantasies would fill her precious early mornings, the time when she felt most energetic and when intended to write a few pages every day. As she noticed the light that had been left on all night she swore quietly at herself: "Damn!"

She sprang out of bed and stood on the floor, inhaling the breeze that was coming in through the window.

A small parcel caught her eye. She picked it up gently, opened it and saw that it contained the pink blouse. Like a drunk she now remembered everything, everything that had happened the night before. The blouse fell to the floor as she unfolded the letter. Her fingers tore the paper into two halves that fluttered away.

"What a ridiculous sentiment," she said softly. "I'm still living blindly, unconsciously. I mustn't live the way other people imagine I do. I must keep a firm grasp on things and move forward correctly and resolutely. I can't go on like this, in this completely worthless way of living."

Grabbing a large towel she ran lightly and fast downstairs to the tap.

The paper was on her table. She had still only written a dozen pages and had just reached the part where the peasant girl Little Sister and the student Miss Tertia were sitting in front of the local god's shrine and talking about things that had happened in their childhood. She now carried on writing, describing how Big Brother was repairing a field dike nearby, standing barefoot in the paddy field with his sleeves rolled high. He was a strong, healthy young man. When they shouted to him he did not answer because he did not know what to say in reply. He was dimly feeling a pain that he could not put into words. . . .

Having taken the story that far she suddenly turned round to see the baby's blouse lying pathetically on the floor. She sighed and turned back to her work.

"Hypocritical rationality! You want to destroy human nature. . . .

"Very well then. Perhaps I'm still wrong. . . ."

With that she went on writing. She was already on page 15.

1933

The Hamlet

THE sun had just gone down behind the hills that faced the door. The trees on them had turned dark and heavy and were clearly etched against the luminous sunset crimson of the sky. Little Sister, who was just fourteen, was standing under a peach tree by the threshing-floor, her face blossom-pink in the evening light. As she gazed at all the beauty that was about to disappear her heart was as bursting with joy as ever. Startled by an impatient sigh she jerked her head round to see a quick-featured woman in her forties standing under a willow nearby, the tender fronds brushing against her shoulders.

"Mum, what are you sighing again for?" she asked anxiously.

Her mother glanced at her before looking back into the distance and saying, as if to herself, "I'm worried."

Little Sister followed her mother's gaze and saw the shapes of two men walking away from them on a distant path between the paddy fields. The taller and stronger one walking behind she recognized as her father. Each raised path was a narrow single line, but there were many of them and the chequered pattern they made was beautiful. The nearby paddy fields stretched out evenly, gleaming with a hint of purple.

"Who's that in front?" she asked. "He's wearing a long padded gown."

"It's Gao Sheng from the master's place. If he's come it must be because he's up to something. I'm scared. It's planting time."

Little Sister did not take her mother's worries too seriously. She still felt happy as she looked at the beautiful field paths that had all been created by the skill of her father and her big brothers. She watched her father and Gao Sheng walking slowly down the little valley and remembered how Gao Sheng looked as refined as a young gentleman with his skinny white hands and those lustreless eyes that had such a horrible way of looking at you.

"That Gao Sheng is disgusting," she found herself saying to her mother, "but you're always buttering him up. I bet Dad's taking him out for a drink. But Big Sister tells me he's just the master's servant. He's a nobody, not even as good as we are."

"You wouldn't understand. The master likes him and follows his advice. He could very easily do us a lot of harm, but he's not a bad sort and he can be buttered up, not like Sanxi. Your big sister's too fond of running people down. You shouldn't be saying things like that."

"She doesn't like running people down. I think it's just that she doesn't like the master's people."

It was dusk by now, and the breeze was turning cool. Her mother turned to go back in, calling, "Go inside, Little Sister, it's cold out there. See how Big Sister is getting on with the meal and lend her a hand."

Little Sister went skipping into the kitchen, which was to the left. She was beginning to feel hungry. The younger of her brothers, who was sitting on a stool outside the kitchen washing his feet, caught her with one arm as she came running over and shouted, "Where are you going?"

"None of your business," she said, struggling to get free. "I'm going to look after the food."

"It's already on the table in the main room. We're just waiting for Dad to get back," said Big Sister in a loud voice from the kitchen.

"He won't be back for supper." She turned away and hurried over to the main room. "Hurry up, Sister. Don't wait for Little Brother."

"You little devil. And you're still not wearing a jacket cover," he shouted in the direction of her green cotton-padded jacket as he deftly lifted a powerful leg and wiped it with a blue cloth. A paraffin lamp stood on the table, its light catching Granny's white hair as she sat beside it. Mother was telling her about Gao Sheng's visit.

"Can't bear the sight of him, sickly little brute," Granny mumbled. "It was much better in the old days under the old master.... If he gives us any more trouble the older boy can carry me into town the very next day and I'll sort it out with the old master's lady. If he won't carry me, I'll walk. I still know the way.... Haven't been to town for nigh on fifteen years."

"All right, Gran, I'll carry you in tomorrow," said Big Brother with a grin, "and we can have a bloody good long look at the operas they're putting on. Mao the Loom-maker came back from town yesterday saying that it's a really good show this time — lots of companies performing, even some bloody girl students who sing with no clothes on. They must be bloody frozen."

"I'm not having you going with that mechanic Mao. He's always going into town. Doesn't work in the fields or weave cotton. Must be a bad lot. But Mao the Third is all right. He behaves himself and knows his place. Why aren't you friends with him?"

"He came here yesterday. We had a bit of a talk at the edge of the hamlet. Do you think he behaves himself? Oh no, he knows what he's about. You'll see one day, he's got it all worked out. He's far ahead of his big brother the loom-maker. All he's got is a loom standing idle."

Little Sister thought of the great black cotton-loom in the loom-maker's house.

"What year was Big Brother born in?" Granny asked Mum. "Yes, he was born in the year of the Monkey, so he must be twenty-one this year. Time to find him a wife."

"I don't want a wife, and I couldn't support one anyhow. We don't want any idle mouths in this family."

"What's the problem?" shouted Little Brother as he came over. "Marry Little Sister off at the same time and we'd be quits."

Little Sister rushed at him and was going to hit him when he gleefully ran round the table shouting, "You're the one that'll get married, you're the one. Not Big Sister."

Just then Big Sister came in with a dish of rice gruel. She stopped Little Sister and asked her brother what he'd said.

He answered in a weak, quiet voice, "I was teasing Little Sister."

"He was saying things about you too," she put in.

"Ignore him. He'd never dare." When Big Sister put the gruel on the table they all began their evening meal. The whole family was afraid of her, but they all loved her too. She loved the whole family, was the hardest worker of them all, and cheerfully toiled away for every one of them.

It was a simple meal — a green dish of rape-seed leaves and a black one of pickled turnips — but it was delicious. The rice was very good, and they all ate with great pleasure, especially Big Brother, who tucked it away at an alarming rate. Big Sister ate the least, only three bowlfuls. Because Granny's teeth were no good any more she always liked gruel, which Little Sister and the rest of them were not keen on. Only solid rice made them feel full.

Before the meal was over Dad slipped quietly back, sat at the table, and asked Little Brother to get him a big bowl of rice. "What happened?" Mum asked with great anxiety. "Why didn't you eat out?"

"Gao Sheng wanted to walk back tonight and be home by tomorrow morning."

"Why's he in such a hurry? What's up?"

Dad's ruddy face showed a touch of worry. "He said that Miss Tertia is going to be sent back to the village tomorrow on the master's orders."

This news astonished them all. Things like this rarely happened. Mother thought for a while then said, "They must be fighting again in town."

Little Sister remembered what had happened many years earlier when she was still a little girl. Miss Tertia and her two older sisters had come to the village with their sister-in-law to keep away from the soldiers. Miss Tertia had been ever such a pretty and kind girl. She'd been so good to Big Sister and nice to her too. Nobody in the village who'd seen Miss Tertia had anything but a good word for her. She had a really pretty face and a plait that anyone would be jealous of. Little Sister jogged her elder sister's elbow and said quietly, "No harm in a bit of fighting."

Her elder sister also looked pleased as she asked, "Will she definitely come tomorrow?"

"I didn't hear Mao the Loom-maker say there was fighting," said Big Brother, who also seemed to be smiling inside.

"The fighting's already over," said Dad, leaving it at that as he filled himself a second bowl of rice.

"But Miss Tertia's almost nineteen," said Mother with incomprehension. "She must be even better looking by now. Why hasn't she married into the Zhao family yet? Is she coming all by herself?"

"She is, and it's a big worry. The master keeps telling Gao Sheng to give me instructions. I really don't understand. That girl. . . ." Dad looked gloomy.

"What about her?" Everyone wanted to hear.

"Some other time," said Dad, looking at Mum. "I only hope she doesn't cause any trouble when she's with us. I don't want a word about all this to anyone, boys, do you understand? Don't you forget."

2

Little Sister went to the pond with Big Sister and squatted on a boulder. Some ducks swam quietly towards them. The sun was shining on the tops of the trees, and the blue sky could be seen in the ripples on the water. White clouds were drifting across it. While her elder sister took a big pile of clothes out of her basket to wash, the younger girl watched the sky being broken up in the water. She'd had nothing of her own to do all day, and had been following her sister around for hours. There was so much she wanted to say to Big Sister, but she was usually too busy to listen. Now Little Sister felt the time was ripe, so she looked her in the face and said, "I'm ever so pleased we're going to have a visitor staying with us tonight. We are, aren't we?"

"I'm very pleased about it too," said Big Sister, moving slightly as she bent over her washing. "But I wonder if she'll still know us."

"She's bound to. You don't look any different. Lots of people say you're prettier than ever. But she might well have forgotten me. She was always your friend before."

"Friend? You shouldn't say that. She might not have time for us any more. She's a young lady. We were just kids messing around together last time. Besides, I don't want to be friends with any young lady."

Little Sister, who did not understand what the older girl was getting at, gazed at the peach blossoms on the other side of the pond as she went on, "I remember what fair, soft skin she used to have. She used to blush whenever anyone said something nice about her. Everybody thought that made her prettier than ever."

"Yes, she does have fair, delicate skin. Young ladies from town are all like that."

"But you're ever so lovely too." Little Sister looked at her sister's regular features, to which the sun had given touches of red and brown, and at her strong, round arms. She had big eyes and a wide forehead, which gave her a rather serious air.

"Don't talk such nonsense," said Big Sister with a

hint of a smile as she listened to the other girl's compliments.

The two of them fell silent while the stick pounded the washing on the boulder. Snatches of a song drifted across from far away.

> Yellow flowers the cabbage in March.
> Sister slips away to see her man. . . .

"Just listen to Big Brother singing." Little Sister ran up the bank to look around, her right hand raised to her forehead. Amid the bluish green of the trees was the fresh green of new leaves. She did not know why she suddenly felt so happy as she shouted, "He's right outside the valley. He must be crazy, singing as loud as that. I want to go and find him."

She skipped as she ran along the path between the low hills, where new grass was sprouting, and the big paddy fields. Thorns stretched across the path caught her, so that she had to sit on the hillside as she untangled herself from several barbed plants. She found herself singing.

> Roses are red,
> And I love you. . . .

"Where are you, Little Sister?" shouted Mum from the threshing-floor.

She came skipping back: she hardly ever walked properly.

"Go to the larder and fetch a piece of smoked pork — the one we've started already. Wash it and get Big Sister to simmer it." Mum was sitting on a little stool patching Dad's old lined jacket.

Little Sister was almost laughing aloud when she thought of the visitor who'd be coming that night. So many people were always saying how beautiful she was. "I wonder what way she's beautiful. Perhaps she's like one of the shell fairies in Granny's stories. Or maybe she's like a fox spirit. I'm sure she's a real stunner, and that her hair must be even blacker and glossier than it was before. That plait of hers. . . ." She sighed sadly as she brushed her own short bunches.

"I wonder if a young lady like her — a fairy — would be able to eat this?" She was standing on a bench to fetch the dirty, black piece of meat down. "It's filthy." She jumped down. "I wonder what she'll be wearing. I remember she had embroidered shoes before."

Little Sister was making up fantasies on the basis of her ordinary life and some oddly assorted fragments of mythology. She painted the heroine of her fantasies in strange and lurid colours, but she was very pleased with the results. Big Sister was even busier than ever getting the room ready for the guest they were expecting. Little Sister's excitement was increased when she learnt that their visitor would be staying in the same room as her and her sister. Granny, who often coughed at night, was being moved into the boys' room. But Big Sister said that Miss Tertia would not necessarily want to share with them. If she didn't, then the two sisters would also have to go in with the boys, or else sleep with the pickled vegetables and the pork in the larder.

After they had waited for Miss Tertia all day and it was now getting dark, Little Sister ran towards the mouth of the little valley, thinking of supper, of her father's low spirits, and of the heroine of her fantasies.

There was not a sound to be heard. In the dusk it was getting hard to make out the shapes of the trees. She was still feeling a little anxious and depressed as she hurried away along the path. She could still see the yellow lamplight from home when she was far away. As she kept turning back to look she thought she could almost see Grandma sitting beside the lamp while Dad smoked his pipe and mother stitched soles for cloth shoes, or else folded up clothes into a neat pile. Only when she looked in front again did she realize that she was already at the back of the little shrine to the local god. Jumping over a ditch, she heard the sound of water flowing gently under her feet. Then she stood under the huge elm tree that gave shelter to the shrine, a clump of honeysuckle and four-o'clock, that little piece of land, the corner of a paddy field, and now her too. All around were beautiful paddy fields, big and small. The water was flowing quietly into some of them; others had just been ploughed, and the earth turned to lie in moist rows. As she gazed all around her Little Sister wondered, "Why isn't she here yet?"

Suddenly she saw a dark shape move. The shock almost made her scream. She ran away for a few paces then stood still and shouted, "Who are you, hiding over there?"

The black shape moved again then said, "It's me, little one, don't be afraid, it's me."

"Oh!" Her heart, which had been pounding wildly, relaxed. "It's you," she laughed as she ran towards it. "You scared me half to death." She pressed herself against her brother.

Big Brother said nothing but just put an arm round her waist. Her heart was still pounding as she took a stealthy look behind her and whispered, "I thought the local god had come out."

Her big brother grunted, held her a little tighter and said, "You mustn't rush about all over the place from now on. You get scared too easily. You always need Mum to calm you down."

This reminded her of what had happened when she had been delirious in a fever. Her mother and elder sister had been so desperate that they had gone out holding the lantern and her clothes to look for her in all her favourite haunts, calling out her name all the way. She recalled how as the distant shouts came closer her mother's plaintive call had been first. "Come back, Little Sister! Is she back yet?" This had been answered by her elder sister's stronger voice, "Come back, Little Sister!" Then the two of them had shouted together, "Little Sister, come back!" After all this she had been much better the next day. She found the thought funny, and asked, "Why's Mum like that?"

"She thinks you were scared out of your wits. Mum really loves Little Sister." It occurred to her that everyone in the family was very fond of her as she pressed even closer to the young man. She looked at his face, felt she ought to show him a little more warmth, took his hand and asked him with a squeeze of it, "Why were you sitting there all by yourself?"

Feeling his hand go limp, she then said, "I want an answer."

Her brother's eyes were far away as he replied, "No reason. I just thought it would be a nice place to sit. Go back now. What did you come here for anyway?"

"No. I won't go back unless you come with me." She too was gazing into the distance, which was now black.

"I came out to meet Miss Tertia. Dad said she's bound to come tonight."

The silence began. Her brother said nothing else to her as he sat there without moving. She began to feel rather depressed again. She was very sorry for her brother, though she did not know why. She felt that something was making him miserable. She tugged at him imploringly and said, "Brother."

The silence continued. She waited for a long while, then began to feel frightened. Her heart was gradually turning as dark and empty as the night. Just when this was becoming unbearable she felt him make a sudden movement.

"Why did you do that?" she exclaimed involuntarily.

"No reason. Go back now." He was calm again.

"No...." Before she had finished her sentence a light appeared on the hill opposite their hamlet. Sometimes it disappeared, probably because a tree was in the way, but a little later it was always back again, gleaming. She felt that her dreams were soon going to come true. "She's here," she said happily. "I'm sure her sedan-chair is behind that lantern."

Ignoring her, her brother gave a low whistle.

The light was slowly getting nearer. It had already come down the hillside, so that nothing was obscuring it now.

"Yes, she's here," Little Sister said. "Let's go back and tell Mum."

But the man beside her was still whistling very quietly. She thought she heard something, the sound of voices carried by the wind. Had there been a moon that night she'd have been able to see who it was. She tugged frantically at her brother.

He just took up a more comfortable stance and roared, "Go home, and take your hands off me. I'm staying here." Then he started his low whistles again.

So she went skipping and running back home by herself. She could hear footsteps as the light came closer than ever.

Once back at the threshing-floor, she shouted, "Mum!"

"Where've you been running off to, little girl?" Little Brother jumped at her from inside the house. "Mum! Dad!" she went on shouting. "She's here! Miss Tertia's here!"

They all rushed out. She went straight over to her mother, who held her hands and said, "They're frozen, silly thing."

Big Sister lit another lamp and came out. The three brown dogs followed them to the cassia tree. Little Sister could see that they were already at the shrine when the low white wall was lit up for a moment by the light of their lantern.

"Is that you, Gao Sheng?" Dad shouted.

"How are you, Zhao Desheng? Been getting impatient?" It was Gao Sheng's voice. Dad then asked, "Why are you so late?"

"Well. . . ."

The dogs were all barking as they ran up to the new arrivals. Little Sister huddled under her mother's arm, watching with anxiety. Mum called the dogs off as she went forward to meet them. She saw Gao Sheng lead the way in carrying the lantern. Behind him walked a slightly-built figure in a long gown, who was followed only by a burly, barefoot fellow carrying something. She tugged at her mother in disappointment and said, "Ask him.   Ask Gao Sheng why she hasn't come."

Before Mum could say anything the slight figure stepped briskly over to her and said, "It's Mrs Zhao, isn't it? How are you?"

They were all astonished by the voice. "Gracious, it's you, Miss Tertia," Mum said. "Why did you walk here?" Big Sister came over, and the lamp lit up Miss Tertia's face.   Her two dark eyes sparkled, and her short hair fell forward over her forehead. She squeezed Big Sister's hand and said with a laugh, "It's Cassia."

Little Sister was too shy at first to look as she hid behind her mother's back but she went closer later. So many people were talking that she could not make out what was being said, and she was too confused to be able to say anything herself.   This came as a complete surprise. Miss Tertia was dressed like a man.

3

It was light. The cocks were still crowing in their coops. Who was it walking around in the main room? Oh, it was Big Brother opening the door.   Her father was up too and smoking.   Little Sister had been awake for ages, curled up in her quilt and not making a sound. Her older sister was getting dressed and slipping out of bed when she noticed that Little Sister's eyes were wide open.   She couldn't help smiling as she said under her voice, "No noise, d'you understand? I'm going to the kitchen." Little Sister looked at the opposite bed, from which came a very light sound of breathing. Before it had all been dreams and fantasies. Little Sister had never imagined she'd be like that, even more amazing than could have been expected. She wasn't at all stuck-up, grand, or even beautiful. She wasn't a bit like a young lady or a fairy, though she was quite attractive. Little Sister thought she was adorable, even more so than in her fantasies, and ever so easy to make friends with. Little Sister felt that her mother and elder sister both liked her. Even her father didn't seem all that gloomy and he liked talking about things in town with her. They all felt completely unconstrained with her, forgetting that she was a young lady. It was just as if she were an old friend.

Someone came into the room, fetched something and went out again. "It's Mum. No, it must be Little Brother," Little Sister thought. "He'll be in trouble for rushing in like that. He ought to realize he might wake her up. She told me herself yesterday she was too tired to sleep. I could hear that it took her ages and ages to get to sleep. I wonder why she was tossing and turning something terrible. Must have been the bedbugs biting her. But it's the wrong time of year for them."

The sun rose. The weather was going to be good again today. When Little Sister poked her head out of her bedding for a look she could restrain herself no longer. She jumped out of bed, dressed as quickly as she could, and was just about to rush out when a voice stopped her, "Wait for me and we'll go together. Will you take me to the kitchen for a wash, Little Sister?"

She looked round and saw that Miss Tertia's head and shoulders had emerged from inside the mosquito-net. "I suppose I'm much too late up." She looked at something on her wrist.

"No. Mum said that you ought to have a good lie in.

You had that long ride in a sedan-chair and a seven-mile walk on top of it yesterday. Then you were much too late going to sleep — it must have been after midnight. You said yourself how tired you were."

Miss Tertia jumped out of bed. Her feet were quite bare. She really was strange.

They went along the passage to the kitchen. Someone was still snoring in her brothers' room. Little Sister took a sidelong glance and saw that the disgusting Gao Sheng had his mouth wide open. He looked really awful. Big Sister had already warmed a big pan of water and was cooking rice in the other pan. They could see her with her head bowed in the smoke and steam making little bundles of straw for the fire. She evidently had not yet had time to do her hair, which was all over the place. Miss Tertia looked all around then said, "Tell me how to do it so I can help you."

"You wouldn't be able to. Besides, it's very dirty here. You go back to your room. I'll send Little Sister along with your water. You can't have had enough sleep last night."

"Of course I did. The air here's wonderful. I feel marvellous." She looked out through the doorway at the countryside. Then she said hesitantly to Big Sister, just like a small child, "I don't want to wash. I want to go out for a look round, is that all right? When do you have breakfast?"

"Of course you can," said Big Sister. "Little Sister'll take you."

She hurried out, closely followed by Little Sister. They went to the pond, to the hillside, to the path she had come along the previous night, and along the narrow little dikes between some paddy fields. She looked avidly all around, breathing heavily, and gazed at Little Sister's innocent face as she said, "How lucky you are."

Little Sister couldn't understand what she meant, and laughed uncomprehendingly. Then she held Miss Tertia's hand tightly and took her towards the mouth of the little valley. On a distant hill a patch of red caught the sunlight. "Such a lot of flowers you have here," she said. "I remember it was spring the last time I came. Memories of those happy days keep coming back to me. What an amazing thing it is to be here again. You were such a tiny thing then, Little Sister. I was always picking you up. It must have been six or seven years ago. Nothing has changed here." When she turned back to look, the house struck her as rather dilapidated. But from another point of view it only set the landscape off even better. The calm, black old tiles and walls, the beautiful thatched side buildings, and the clean and pleasing colour of the low yellow clay walls. The cottage was shielded by many tall trees and the gentle slopes of the spurs of the hill, and the beautiful countryside was spread out in front like a picture. To her it seemed like a lost paradise away from the world's troubles.

Little Sister saw her father with his hand on the harrow as he turned it, shouting at the water-buffalo.

"Hey!" she called. Dad waved at them with his whip as the buffalo stumbled laboriously across some uneven lumps of earth. He had to stand on the harrow to break them up. "That's my dad," Little Sister told her happily.

They both stood and watched the big buffalo pulling the weight of a strongly-built man. Then Dad shouted at the animal as before to drive it along.

"My goodness. What a marvellous dad to have. You have such a lovely family."

The thought of the whole family made Little Sister feel happier than ever.

They did not want to go, so they stood there for quite a while before Little Sister said, "Let's find somewhere to sit down."

They went over to the big elm where Little Sister had waited for her the previous night. As Little Sister remembered last night and all her imaginings she found herself staring at Miss Tertia again. She looked prettier than she had last night. She really was rather fair, but she shouldn't have had that glossy black plait cut off, and she shouldn't be wearing that man's long blue cotton gown. Her shoes weren't right either. "Yes, I remember it here. We played here lots of times. I used to hide here when we played hide-and-seek. What terrific fun we had." She sprang down to the local god's shrine and took a close look at the two little foot-high clay figures. "They're just the same as before," she said to Little Sister with a smile. Then she searched all over the wall for a long time before saying with an air of disappointment, "Someone must have rubbed it out, and it seems to have been rubbed out recently. I'm sure I remember writing something here before."

A rook flew from a branch, making it wave gently. Little Sister said to her with a smile, "In a couple of days this tree will rain fruit. Do you believe me?"

"Yes."

They sat where Little Sister had sat with Big Brother the previous night. She gazed into the distance, lost in thought, while Little Sister gazed at her with affection and an air of mystery.

There were noises behind them, noises of mud splashing into water. Little Sister looked round, lightly touched her and whispered, "Look! It's him! My eldest brother."

She would never have recognized the naughty boy who used to look after the water-buffalo in this strapping, barelegged, young peasant with his sleeves rolled up. How often she had ridden his buffalo with him. She had usually needed to be lifted on or off a buffalo, but he could do it just by springing up or down. She remembered the old days again and all the games they had played. Then she thought of the buffalo and found herself asking Little Sister, "Who looks after that buffalo now? Does he still?"

"No, he's grown up. He helps Dad to plough, and Dad says he's as strong as two buffaloes. Dad likes him a lot. Actually, he's more capable than Dad. Even Little Brother can work in the fields now. There's no one else to look after the buffalo now. Sometimes I take it out, but Mum won't let me go very far. She says that when Big Brother was little he used to take it much too far away. He got bitten several times by vicious dogs."

They looked at him bent over the field dike he was repairing, unaware that there were people so near him.

Little Sister called to him. He looked up in surprise then bent down again. He neither would nor could reply to them.

"I'd still recognize him. His face and manner haven't changed. He's just grown. Why didn't I see him last night? I'm sure I didn't."

"But last night he. . . ."

Big Sister was calling from under the cassia tree by their front door. Little Sister jumped up.

"Let's go back. Breakfast time."

"Let's go back with Big Brother."

"Over here, Big Brother. Come back with us."

He ignored his sister and kept his head bowed low.

They walked over to him and stood on a frighteningly narrow field dike he had just repaired. Only then did he look up and say hastily, "Don't come this way. You might fall in."

"Zhao Jinlong!" Miss Tertia called.

Both hands plastered with mud and his feet deep in the water, Big Brother walked towards them without saying anything.

"You didn't recognize me," Miss Tertia said.

He gazed at her face under her bobbed hair, still saying nothing. As he walked ahead of them, his wet feet left footprints behind him. His white cotton trousers were rolled up very high, and his black cotton waistcoat did not cover his arms, which were a reddish colour. Little Sister was growing a little cross with him for saying nothing. "Idiot," she said, then went on to add, "but really he's smashing."

Miss Tertia only smiled.

He set off briskly straight towards the kitchen, not waiting for them.

Miss Tertia did not see the boys and their father during breakfast, and only found out later that they had taken their meal sitting in front of the stove, staying outside because they were too dirty for the young lady. They were not let in for other meals either. The girls said that the boys were too rough and didn't know how to behave themselves.

Gao Sheng had now gone. When he went he said he would be back in a few days and bring the young lady any food or clothes she needed. But she did not ask him to bring anything and was very cold with him. She showed no signs at all of missing home. Gao Sheng must have said something else to Little Sister's father, because when Dad came back for dinner he seemed to be trying to hide something as he said to the young lady, "Miss Tertia, I'm sure you understand a lot. Just stay in the hamlet. Little Sister'll look after you. Things aren't what they used to be in the countryside now. People's hearts aren't in the right place. There are wicked people everywhere."

"Don't worry, Mr Zhao," she replied openly. "I understand. That Gao Sheng is a rat. Don't pay any attention to him."

Little Sister did not know or even want to know what all this was about. It was enough that she could be with Miss Tertia all day. Mother had told her that the only thing she had to do was to look after Miss Tertia all the time.

But in fact nothing happened to worry the family, and they were happier than ever. She did not stand on her dignity at all and was ever so easy-going, treating them all as if they were her own brothers and sisters. She was alarmingly mischievous, telling stories that made them all laugh at mealtimes, when she refused to allow the boys to eat separately in the kitchen. At first Zhao Desheng, the father of the family, had felt uneasy about all this and insisted on having the young lady treated with more respect, but even he had gradually got used to it, and gazed at her with adoration. He regarded her as really a child hardly any older than Little Sister although she could make you forget your exhaustion with all her stories and explanations of so many things. She was always helping them in their work. She could thresh rice and make the soles for cloth shoes, and when she had made one she would hold it up with a smile before throwing it down. She could even put up with Granny, and for a town girl to put up with a country granny was something almost unheard of.

"There's something a bit fishy about that Gao Sheng," was what Zhao Desheng finally thought. Then he dropped the idea because he felt that he should not have any more suspicions or funny ideas. If she could stay on with them that would be the best and most natural thing to happen.

4

By a lucky chance the weather got better every day. Light showers would often fall during the night, but from dawn onwards the sun shone. The breeze was slightly cool, slightly humid, and slightly scented with young grass. The hills, the trees and the fields were a brighter green than ever; and the sky was even more clear, translucent and powdery blue. Although the work here was heavy it was still a place in which to forget one's troubles. The family felt that life was rather more easy for them than it had been in the past. In the first place, Gao Sheng had come from town with some smoked fish and pork, so that they often ate some meat thanks to the young lady. There were more vegetables in the vegetable patch now that the young lady and Little Sister were lending a hand. Secondly, most of the planting was over, so they no longer had that on their minds; and the good weather had freed them from worries about disasters of that sort. In addition they were having a lot more fun. They had someone to listen to their family gossip, to the toil and hardship of their lives and to their pitiful pleasures. Not only did Miss Tertia listen: she replied, wanted to ask more and to explain why they laboured for no return, and gave them ideals and the hope that they could be realized. She taught them and spurred them on. But they still saw her as an adorable child because she could not help slipping into being mischievous all the time, so that they laughed, forgot who she was, and wanted to hit, stroke or even hug her.

Little Sister was with her all day looking so happy; the two of them did all the little jobs about the house. She got up early at the same time as the rest of them and while the three men went out carrying their heavy loads, Big Sister cooked the rice and Mum tidied the house up, the two of them would open up the chicken coops and count the seven hens. They also kept a very good eye on the five ducks, none of which they lost to a weasel. They also went to see the pigs, which were growing well. These were creatures that did not need a lot of money spent on them. Sometimes they led the water-buffalo out and sometimes they liked to watch it lying in its pen and eating the grass. They also went to the vegetable patch to pick the vegetables to be eaten, sprinkle the patch with some liquid fertilizer, and hunt for bugs. Little Sister told her how to do all sorts of jobs, even ordering her about at times, which did not seem at all odd to either of them. When they had some free moments they would go to the pond to play with the water or watch the rice being transplanted outside the village. Big Brother had recently taken a liking to working in the fields nearest to home, sometimes even just outside the house, so that they were in sight of each other as they worked. When they called to him he would answer, and if he started a song Little Sister would take it up. Little Sister taught Miss Tertia to sing their songs, which made her laugh; and Little Sister laughed when Miss Tertia taught her songs. They had ever such funny words that Little Sister passed on to her brothers, who weren't at all afraid to sing them when they were working, walking or washing their feet — noble and stirring songs.

Such was the happiness and excitement in which they lived, oblivious of everything else, that they did not realize that she had been with them for nearly ten days when she and Little Sister led the water-buffalo to eat the grass on the hill opposite. They lay on the grass near the buffalo while Little Sister told her stories about the Wild Old Witch. Little Sister did not notice that there was something different about Miss Tertia today as she restlessly kept sitting up then lying down again. When Little Sister happened to look in her direction she said, as if nothing was up, "Go on. What happened next?" Whereupon Little Sister carried on with the story, gazing at the changing pictures in the clouds.

Later Miss Tertia climbed into the fork of a tree and said to Little Sister lying on the grass, "I can hear from here. I like the way you tell the story and I want to know how it ends."

The sunshine had made Little Sister feel rather tired. She shut her eyes and answered, "Didn't the older sister trip her up with a rope in the tree and make her fall to her death?"

"Yes, that's right."

The buffalo was grazing and some bees flew over. Little Sister opened her eyes but did not want to get up from the grass where she was lying. "I can see a big clump of azaleas over there," she said to Little Sister. "You stay here while I go and pick some."

Little Sister sat up and looked all around. "Where? I'll come with you. I can't see any."

"There are, it's just that you haven't seen them. I'm going over to have a look. You wait for me here and watch the buffalo. I'll soon be back whether I find them or not, then we can go home together. I expect Big Sister's looking out for us."

Little Sister hesitated for a moment, saw that the buffalo still had its head down and was pulling at the grass, turned over and lay down again.

"All right. Hurry up. Call me if you find some and I'll lead the buffalo over."

Miss Tertia slipped down from her tree and ran off, shouting back as she went, "Wait there for me. I'll be back straight away."

Little Sister watched as she ran down the hillside and into a clump of big trees that hid her completely "There can't possibly be any azaleas there," Little Sister thought. "She's wasting her time. There are plenty on the hills behind the house." Little Sister looked back up at the sky, from which the clouds had all disappeared, leaving a vast ocean overhead. The buffalo was eating the tender grass for all it was worth, and still she had not come back. Little Sister waited patiently.

The time passed, and Little Sister only began to feel worried when she heard her elder brother calling. She looked for Miss Tertia everywhere but could not find any sign of her; she shouted but got no reply. It was rather difficult to look for her when leading the buffalo, but Little Sister searched as best she could on the way home until she found Big Brother in the paddy field next to the house.

"Have you seen her?"

"Who? No, I haven't."

"She pretended she was going to pick azaleas, but she didn't come back. I don't know where she's gone."

"I'll go and look for her," said Big Brother, then laughed. He added that Miss Tertia had probably gone back to the house as a joke. He told Little Sister to go home herself then went on with his work.

Once back at the house Little Sister searched high and low, still without finding a sign of her. Big Sister and Mum both said that they had not seen her come back and told Little Sister off. Then everyone rushed outside and started shouting, at which Big Brother yelled, "I said she was only teasing Little Sister. I saw her going up the hill at the back a moment ago. If you don't believe me, go home — she'll be there before you."

Big Brother insisted repeatedly that he had not been mistaken: she had looked funny rushing around under the trees. They hurried back to the house to find her washing her face, which was bright red, in the kitchen. She was panting heavily and smiling at them, but she did not say anything. Little Sister grabbed hold of her and complained, "Why did you trick me? You were nearly the death of me. I looked for you everywhere. Didn't you hear me shouting?"

At this she burst out laughing and said, "I heard you and I saw you coming back. I did it deliberately as a tease."

"You shouldn't have. You ran away from me for far too long."

When Mum saw two thorn scratches that were still bleeding on her hands she bandaged them for her. "Look at you," Mum said with a sigh, "you're such a child."

"All right, I won't go rushing off again." She gave Mum a look of such winning charm that everybody burst out laughing.

For several days she did not in fact go out, but on the fourth day Little Sister came back from feeding the pigs to find her gone. Little Sister thought that she must be at the vegetable patch, but she was not there. Mum, who was sitting in the sun outside the front door making shoe soles, had not seen her; and Big Sister had not noticed her while washing the clothes in the pond. Granny said she could not possibly be in the house as she had not heard a sound for ages. Little Sister went to all the places they usually went together, but she was not under the trees, among the flowers or anywhere. Little Sister took the road out of the hamlet again only to be told off by her brother for being silly. None of the menfolk had seen her and she had not gone away. Little Sister went back home but she was still not there. When Big Sister joined in the search they went to the hill at the back where the new bamboos had grown tall but there was still no sign of her. They were now starting to feel desperate.

They went to tell their father what had happened, and his anxiety came as even more of a shock. He yelled at Little Sister, "I'll kill you, you useless fool. I told you to watch her, didn't I? Why the hell did you let her get away by herself?" Then he roared, "When you go back say nothing, stay at home and get on with your jobs. I'm going to take a look in the fields before going back." He picked his coat up from the field dike, threw it over his shoulders, took his pipe and set off. All the girls could do was wait quietly.

Finally she came home with Dad. He was under a cloud of deep gloom and said not a word before going back to the fields. She was smiling, and said that she had lost her way and kept going round in circles when she tried to come back. She was in a particularly amiable mood because she realized she had caused the family so much worry. Little Sister, who had been in trouble and been told off because of her, was so far from being angry with her that she felt a great deal of sympathy for her. Dad's unconcealed distress seemed rather repulsive to Little Sister, who even felt apologetic towards her.

"Where did you really go?" she asked her in a whisper. "Tell me next time you go out and I'll go with you. I know all the paths for six or seven miles around."

Miss Tertia sighed. "I'm tired out. Let me rest. I won't run off again. Tell them to stop worrying. It doesn't matter at all. It's not important."

After they had eaten that evening — it was not an enjoyable meal as Dad was in a bad mood, no doubt because of what happened during the day — Dad sent the boys and Little Sister to bed. Little Sister did not really want to go, so she lay wide awake for a long time without going to sleep. She could hear Miss Tertia talking and laughing, but in a very sad way as if she were talking about getting lost during the day. Big Sister and Mum replied to her in low voices and gradually changed the subject. Then she could hear her father talking, but too quietly for her to catch what he was saying. Miss Tertia replied, "Don't believe a word of it. Gao Sheng's a bad lot. Look at me. What's wrong with me?"

"Yes," thought Little Sister, "what's wrong with her? Who says there's anything wrong with her?"

Little Sister could not catch what Dad said next, but she heard Miss Tertia putting in, "You know what the master's like. He lies by his opium lamp all day and knows nothing. He believes everything those bastards tell him."

". . . . . ."

"They're all dreadful young gentlemen and they're none of them up to any good. They keep me under guard and their thugs in town won't let me go into town or have a penny of my own. It's all their fault. I've been here long enough for you to know me. Am I as terrible as they say?"

Little Sister couldn't understand how anyone could say she was terrible. Miss Tertia's father? Her brothers? Her servants? Why had they sent her to the countryside? Why was Gao Sheng intimidating Dad? He must have said something to her dad.

Her father was speaking again, and when his voice got louder she could hear him saying, "Anyhow, you ought to realize what danger you're in. They're after you. And it could make a terrible difference to us. Our whole family depends on this place for its living. You know perfectly well that it only needs one of the masters in your family to tell us to go and we'll all be dead. Look, I've got my old mother and. . . ." He said no more.

The main room fell silent, and Little Sister could feel her nostrils tingling. It was a long time before Little Sister heard Miss Tertia's reply.

"You can't go on depending on my family for ever. It's too unreliable. You must be more aware and think of a better way. You're still losing out. Anyhow, don't be anxious about me. I won't go far. I just take my walks around here. There's nothing to worry about."

Later they changed the subject, so Little Sister lost interest and went to sleep.

5

Little Sister was now even less willing than before to let Miss Tertia out of her sight, both because she loved her and because Mum kept on telling her to watch her. Although Little Sister was with her all day, Little Sister felt rather apologetic and resentful of her father on noticing that Miss Tertia looked a little tired. She wished she could let her go further away. "You must be fed up with this place," Little Sister said to her several times. "It's no fun here."

"But I like it here. I don't miss town at all. It's all the same really. But. . . ."

"I'll take you somewhere today you haven't been before. There are lots of birds and mushrooms there, and the cracks in the rocks are full of orchids. The whole hill smells lovely. Let's sneak off there."

She turned Little Sister's offer down with a smile, "No, you're ever so kind, Little Sister. I'll never forget you. You know your father will tell me off if he finds out; he might even send me back to town. If that happened my family could lock me up. They'd never have let me come here if I hadn't given them such a fright."

"Why are they so horrible to you?"

"It's because they want to do wicked things. You don't know them. They're just like tigers or wolves. My mother's the only one who's any different, but she's too weak to be able to do anything. I'm ever so sorry for her."

"Tigers and wolves?" thought Little Sister. "Why does she say they're like tigers and wolves? Tigers and wolves eat people." Then Little Sister said aloud to her, "Dad says your family's very rich, and your house is ever so big. They couldn't be tigers and wolves. The people who live there must all be very kind. They couldn't possibly be cruel!"

Miss Tertia laughed, took Little Sister by the hand and explained to her with a smile, "You're too young to understand much about the world, and you've never been to our town. Although your family is poor, you work hard and are frugal. With good weather and a bit of luck you've been able to get by. You've never left this home where you're loved and everybody is so good and contented with his lot. None of you grumbles or complains. Of course you feel you're happy, and I reckon that you really are, as you've never seen evil and you wouldn't understand it. You'd never realize that only wolves and tigers can live in big houses."

Little Sister thought for a long time but still did not understand much of what she was on about, then said, "My big sister doesn't like your family. She hates them for no reason at all and won't tell us why. Mum's always going on at her about it. Granny thinks Big Sister's too hard on your family as we all depend on you. The old master used to be decent to us and we ought to be grateful to him, but in the last few years even Gran has started to grumble sometimes. Last summer we had to eat broad beans and maize for two whole months because Gao Sheng sent men to take our rice away. Dad was terribly angry about it. All Mum could do was cry. Things got better later. We all worked and forgot about it. After all, as Dad explained, the rice really belonged to your family. It was just that Gao Sheng and his lot were being too hard on us. They should have left us a bit. We've been with your family for dozens of years, and we've never ever done you wrong from your grandfather's time till now. I suppose that you didn't have any rice to eat yourselves then. Dad said that last year's rice was all sold and taken away because the crops failed somewhere far from here."

"There was nothing unusual about what happened. That's why I told you they were all wolves and tigers. It wasn't only your food-grain that they took last year. We have lots of farm-hands, and lots of our land is rented out too. They grabbed rice from wherever they could, and our two rows of granaries were both full up. Later we sold huge quantities when the price was three times as high as normal. What would you know about it? Your father's so good and docile that he deserves what he gets. If I hadn't come here I'd never have believed that there were decent people in the world; but you country people are too good. Why did you accept eating broad beans and maize so calmly?"

"Dad can't be any other way. Dad even treats Gao Sheng with respect but Big Sister has only contempt for him. When Gao Sheng sent those men to grab our rice Dad dared not do anything because he'd obviously have had no hope of winning. Besides, there was no point in asking for so much rice."

"Why wouldn't you have won? Think how many of

you there are. You could set out from here and carry
on and on without ever reaching an end, and everywhere you went the strong and healthy people living in
thatched huts, working in the fields, or beside the
buffalo pens would all be your people."

She said a lot more and enthralled Little Sister with
her patient explanations. Little Sister was so excited
that she ran off to find her brothers so that Miss Tertia
could explain things to them too. The boys were stirred
up by what she said, but neither of them would say a
word. Zhao Desheng had his sons under very good
control.

"Don't pay any attention to her," he kept saying to
them. "Of course she's right, but she's a young lady
and doesn't know how hard life can be. She sees things
differently. Do you realize how difficult everything is?
In the thousands of years since the creation of heaven
and earth this is all people have managed to do. How
can we possibly put the world to rights now? This is the
way our forefathers lived, so what have we got to com-
plain about? I've got a mother, you've got a mother,
and later on you'll be getting married and having
children of your own. Now you can understand why
her family sent her here. She'd been stirring people up
in town just like this. Other people wanted to arrest
her. Gao Sheng said she was a terror. . . . But she's a
good girl and ever so well-behaved. What she says is
true, but I won't have you listening to her."

Zhao Desheng's sons felt that what their father said
was right. They had a good home and were more or
less able to get by, so why shouldn't they be contented?
Anyone in the family who stepped at all out of line

would destroy them all. They had not reached the stage of rising up. The time had not yet come.

But she was rather a charmer, and they all felt closer to her than ever. Mum loved to hold her by the wrist and say, "Why are you so different from the rest of them? If they were all like you the world would be a much better place."

She smiled and patted Mum, and put on a funny imitation of an intimidating expression. "You've forgotten again. You mustn't put your hopes in anyone but yourselves."

The family lived in an atmosphere of excitement that they could not quite explain. It was because they were all now thinking new and more complicated thoughts.

She continued to tell them funny stories and to act very mischievously to make them laugh. Their lives were so hard that they needed a little joy. They never dared to slack off for a moment from dawn till dusk, and they could not either: there was too much to be done, and never enough time. It was wonderful to have her with them, and each of them felt that she was indispensable. They took better care of her than ever and were always being careful on her behalf. They knew why they needed to do so and how to protect her. Little Sister did not realize it yet. She was too young to be cautious. Big Brother kept a quiet eye on her and never let her go outside the hamlet. He had not been out for a long time himself either, although he always used to go for a walk at dusk. Once Big Brother saw someone walking through the trees on the hill behind the house and shouted some abuse at him before going home. He wondered why the man looked rather like Mao the Third. What was he doing here? Then when he got home he saw his elder sister sitting on the steps looking at the sky. She was wearing a white cotton tunic and a blue skirt embroidered with white flowers. He evidently had something in mind when he asked her with a grin, "What are you thinking about, sitting there instead of getting on with your work, my girl?"

"I've only just come here," she replied, looking round at him. "Why shouldn't I take a break? Dad brought back some patterns of cloth shoes to be made up from the market yesterday. He says that ten pairs have to be delivered by the end of the month. We women have a lot to do." She looked back up at the sky, but he only grinned and replied, "Huh! If you've only just come here where did you go before that? Tell me, you little devil."

She looked at him with uncomprehending astonishment, then went back into the house, ignoring him. Big Brother reckoned that he had guessed right and laughed triumphantly. Later he told Little Sister to keep an eye on Big Sister and not let her go running off.

"She never goes running off."

"Don't say anything and just keep an eye on her quietly. Something interesting's happening."

Little Sister did spend a lot of time going about with Big Sister but she did not see anything at all interesting. Big Sister was kept busy all day with three meals, a big basket of washing and shoe soles to stitch if she had any spare time. Miss Tertia helped her to stitch soles. Big Sister liked to talk about her dreams with Miss Tertia. If she were a man, she said, she would have left home long ago. When her younger sister asked where she would go she said with a smile, "You wouldn't understand, and I don't even know myself.

Anyhow, I'd want to do something really terrific to show everybody."

Miss Tertia gazed at her with a smile and said, "I believe you. You're very capable. You should do something.   Men and women are equal."

Big Sister shook her head and said that Miss Tertia did not understand.   Miss Tertia said that it was Big Sister who did not understand and the two of them started an argument that Little Sister really could not follow.   Big Sister usually lost as Miss Tertia could reduce her to helpless silence; when the argument ended she would still be shaking her head, her mind full of troubles she could not resolve.

Big Sister had always been a thinker, and recently her thinking had gone a lot further, as even Granny had noticed: she said that the girl was cracked in the head.

6

One day Little Sister and Miss Tertia went rather a long way from home before Little Sister realized what had happened. Miss Tertia kept producing excuses for leaving Little Sister for a while, but Little Sister saw through them and said with a laugh, "It's no good. I'm going to stay with you all the time. If Dad really lost his temper he'd beat me."

Miss Tertia at first refused to admit that she had been trying to get away, then tried cajoling and finally pleaded, "Honestly, it's a girl from my school who lives at Fishbelly Slope.   She's longing for me to go and see her. She'll probably be a lot better in a few days and able to come visiting us. I'll take you next time, but

today you've really got to wait for me. I'll be back ever
so soon. I just need time for a quick look at her. I'm
worried because she's very ill."

Little Sister did not want to let her go and did not
feel very pleased with her, but could not help feeling
very sorry for her when she put it like that.

"You're a kind girl. Just let me this once. Otherwise
I'll be ever so miserable. What if her illness gets even
worse?"

"Ask Dad first. You can tell him the truth."

"I can't possibly tell him. He'd never let me go unless
I really insisted. You must let me. I beg you to help me.
I like you and you like me. Can't you let me do this
one little thing? You've always been so kind."

Little Sister looked at her and her heart melted. She
leant against the trunk of a tree, gazed into the distance
and said, "Do what you like, but be back as soon as you
can."

"All right. You stay here and don't move." With that
Miss Tertia ran off as fast as she could.

Little Sister was bored wandering around in the
wood. The time passed very slowly and, apart from
feeling worried about Miss Tertia, she was cross with
her for leaving her here. Luckily it was not too long
before she came rushing back, red in the face, pouring
with sweat and so breathless she could say nothing, to
throw herself to the ground in front of her. Little Sister
was astonished, but when asked why Miss Tertia only
shook her head and said, "It's nothing. I just ran a bit
too fast because I was worried you might stop waiting
and go home without me."

Miss Tertia would not take a proper rest but hurried

back home with Little Sister. They were both worried about Miss Tertia's outing being found out.

She did it many more times, and because Little Sister loved her and wanted to stay friends with her she kept her secret.

Once when Little Sister was alone in the wood the sky suddenly became overcast and the pigeons called incessantly. Towards the distant horizon there was thunder and lightning, and the wind was howling. Little Sister was frightened, reckoning that she would not be back for a long time. When Little Sister looked anxiously at the grey sky and the dark clouds scudding across it she began to rush around the wood, desperately worried about what would happen if Miss Tertia did not come straight back. She looked all around, but there was nobody to be seen. The wood was in an isolated valley hemmed in by low slopes and there was a hill between there and home. She felt panicky, but she could not go back and was determined to wait for her, so she sat on a tree trunk and counted the minutes going by. Before long there was a rustling patter as fine rain began to fall on the leaves, and still Little Sister felt there was no hope of her coming back. Birds and other creatures kept moving about in the wood and the sky was frighteningly dark. She started walking about, but it did no good. The rain was becoming heavier, soaking her clothes and her hair. She thought of the panic there was bound to be at home but neither dared nor wanted to go back by herself. The only thing she could do was wait for her, so she found a better place.

Someone's distant shouts were carried to her then cut off again by the wind. She listened hard and realized it was her elder brother calling to her from the other side of the hill. She dared not reply but started feeling miserable and cold.

Still she did not come back.

Big Brother's shouts grew nearer. He was now over the hill. Little Sister could see him, but she dared not make a sound as he came down the hillside, his clothes soaked through. He was shouting and cursing angrily, and although he came close he turned away without seeing her. She could see that he was wearing only thin clothes and had not put on his palm-fibre cloak or bamboo rain-hat. He looked as though he had come out in a hurry the moment he got back from the fields. His clothes were so wet they stuck to him and the rain was blowing straight into his eyes so that he had to keep wiping them with his hand. The sight made her feel so sad and sorry for him that she could not help calling out to him, "Come back, Brother, I'm here."

He turned round and she threw herself into his arms. He swore at her coarsely, then asked in a shocked voice, "Are you here by yourself?"

"Yes. She's gone to see one of the girls at her school who's so ill she's dying. You mustn't tell. I promised her I wouldn't let Dad know."

"I damn well will, and I hope Dad beats you to death." He glared at her.

She clung to him, moaning in a trembling voice.

"All right then," she said after a while. "He can beat me to death if he likes. You go back. I'll wait for her here."

He said nothing for a long time, then put his arms round his sister and led her under the biggest tree in the wood, where they sat on a root, sheltered by the leaning trunk and the heavy foliage from the worst of the rain.

He leant against the tree as she pressed against his wet body weeping until he could take no more and said, "What are you crying for, you little fool? I'm not cross with you."

This only made her sob more bitterly than ever, at which his voice turned harsh again, "Stop it. Now, tell me how it all happened. I don't want any lies. If you're honest with me I won't let Dad know."

She told him everything and kept repeating why she could not have refused to let Miss Tertia go.

He said not a word, and the two of them sat waiting for her in silence. Some rain was still dripping from the trees while the thunder rumbled quietly far from the wood. With her brother beside her Little Sister was not bothered by any of this, though his silent gloom disturbed her. She pressed against him, her own clothes also wet.

They heard someone else calling for Little Sister. Fearing that it might be her elder sister or her other brother she hid behind him, pleading in a whisper, "Keep quiet."

"I'm going to take a look," he said, standing up.

She held on to him refusing to let him go. The mystery was solved at once as Miss Tertia came through the wood behind them, a jacket over her head, her clothes soaking wet and calling Little Sister's name. She showed a touch of astonishment as she looked at the gloomy young man, then hugged Little Sister and said, "I've been terribly anxious about you. That's the only reason I came back. Miss Zhang wouldn't let me go. Look at you. You must have been worried to death, and your clothes are soaked through. Let's go back."

"We can't," said Little Sister. "It's raining harder than ever. Better stay here." Little Sister looked at her brother, and they went back to the place where they had been sitting before.

She was covered in mud, especially her feet. She must have fallen over: there was even mud on her hands and on the jacket over her head. After Little Sister asked Miss Tertia when she had set out back she told them some more details. Big Brother looked at her in a silence that Little Sister found a little frightening. Then he spoke, "Very well, you fooled her. But I know where you were. A couple of days ago I heard people talking about you outside the village and I didn't know what to do. Your name's on the list. If my dad knew what you've been up to he'd drop all his farmwork and take you straight back to the master's place."

"I won't go back. I'd give you the slip."

"I believe you. I won't say anything, but you'd better be careful. There are a lot of bad people around here. You don't know them, but they know who you are."

"I know." She sprang to her feet before continuing, "You're terrific. I'm sure you sympathize with me — with us. Later you'll understand even better and be even firmer. You're one of us. I've always known. Your whole family is marvellous."

He said nothing as he gazed at her trying to hold back whatever he wanted to say.

The rain was easing off as they walked slowly home. Big Brother gave Little Sister a determined look as he said, "We're going home now. Keep your mouth shut. Do you understand?"

"Yes."

She ran back hand-in-hand with the two of them, climbing up and down the slippery hillsides.

7

It was now much less of a secret that Miss Tertia went out. Big Sister and Mum knew, and whenever she went they would go some of the way with her, giving her all sorts of advice. Little Sister no longer had to hide in the wood waiting for her anxiously. She borrowed some of Big Sister's working clothes and wrapped a cloth round her head so that from a distance she looked like a woman out gathering grass for thatching. As she hurried off with a smile mother and daughters started talking about her, from her looks to her character. That was what they liked best about her. Finally they got round to her ideas and to all the things she told them about. They believed everything she taught them. How could a young lady like her know so much about the hard times that peasants like themselves had and about all the rest of the world's suffering? So much was wrong with the world that they were not going to put up with it any longer: they had suffered for long enough. The world ought to be put to rights, and what she was doing was for the sake of everybody, which made them feel more respect for her than ever. That was why they did not oppose her, thought of safer methods for her to use and kept Dad in the dark. As soon as she came back they were eager to know everything, so she would tell them what she had done that day. They were things she cared about deeply.

Big Brother was also clearly aware of the changes that

had taken place in the family recently. He knew what the women were always talking about, that she went out, and who she was planning things with. But he was the last person in the family to give her secrets away as he cared for her and sympathized with her more than any of them, and was himself inclined towards doing that kind of work. He knew rather more than the rest of the family. Mao the Third had talked to him quite often, but he did not dare do anything as he was afraid of his father who was keeping a close eye on him. He was often fed up at the end of a day's work in the fields, but he felt ashamed in her presence. There was so much that he wanted to pour out to her, but he had neither the opportunity nor the courage to do so.

One evening after supper he left the others and went gloomily out of the house. The hills and the fields were bathed in moonlight when he went out into the still of the night, whistling to keep his spirits up on his way to the shrine of the local god. It was such a friendly place. Before long he heard somebody coming along the path, turned and saw two shapes walking slowly towards him. It was Big Sister and Miss Tertia, and he could hear Big Sister saying, "The first thing is to stop the dogs barking. You go round to the back and leave that side-door unbolted. I won't go to sleep. Be careful on the road and come back soon."

He was quite taken aback at the shock of this strange development, then tried carefully to listen to what they said next, but without success as they were talking too quietly.

They walked further away from him and split up at the edge of the hamlet. Big Sister turned back, and he longed to jump out, grab and question her, but she ran home as if on wings. The person outside the hamlet was also making off at high speed. Without being aware of it he jumped to his feet and was after her. He was really worried for her, and as he closed the gap between them she seemed to have heard the noise behind her as she slowed down. But when he caught up with her he did not know what to say. After walking for a while she turned off on to a path and stood there as if waiting for him to go ahead. He stopped too and looked into her eyes that were hidden under her head-cloth. Suddenly she called to him in a low voice, "Oh, it's you. I thought it was someone else. What are you doing here?"

"Nothing, just walking along with you," he mumbled haltingly.

"Fine. Let's go then." She took the lead.

They said nothing for a long time. Then, unable to contain himself any longer, he asked anxiously, "Why are you doing it so late?"

"Yes, the time's been changed. People are too busy in the fields during the day."

"I was worried you'd be scared. You're not used to walking at night."

"It doesn't matter. It's nearer now and I know the way."

They walked further, then she stopped, turned to him and said, "Why don't you come too? They've mentioned you several times: you ought to come along."

A powerful impulse struck his heart. He longed to agree, but he hesitated and replied, "I can't tonight. Perhaps I can in a couple of days. Dad's really against it."

"Never mind. He's bound to see the light before long. You're very useful. You really ought to come."

While he thought she added, "All right then. Go back now. No need for you to come with me."

He hesitated again and asked, "What about when you come back?"

"No problem. I expect one of them will come with me. There'll be no need for you to fetch me."

She hurried off and was soon gone. He stood there gazing at her and feeling miserable, regretting that he had not gone with her. It was a long time before he turned away.

The front door would have been shut long ago, and he thought they must all be asleep. Not daring to go back, he waited till she returned before going in with her through the side-door. He heard Big Sister coughing.

He escorted her this way twice more. The third time he said to her, "I've made my mind up. I've decided not to be afraid of anything."

"I know," she said, turning to him with a smile.

He felt something leap in his heart. "Are you happy?"

She laughed and looked at him again before saying, "Why not? Of course I'm happy. One of my childhood friends is walking hand-in-hand with me along the same path. That's very exciting. Look at you. The naughty boy has turned into someone who understands how people ought to live. If you think what I was like when I was little you must find it very strange too. I must have been a spoilt brat in those days."

He was silent for a long time before he said, "You were never high and mighty, but in those days we only dared play with you. You're even better now. I really admire what you do."

"You still don't understand. It's because we're even closer now. We're 'comrades'."

She looked at him in so friendly a way that he felt excited. The word "comrade" gave him a new and more honourable significance.

Then she started talking about their work in a low voice, explaining many points on which he had his doubts. By now they had passed the point at which they usually separated. She stopped and said to him, "Remember to find some excuse to leave the fields after dinner tomorrow and go to the wood at the back where there'll probably be someone looking out for you. Don't worry about your dad. I can see very clearly that he'll be no problem."

He had another premonition of happiness. "I'll wait for you all the same," he said. "Here will do."

"No, I might be a bit later back tonight. Big-mouth Zhang from over the hill will see me back. He comes the same way as far as the edge of the hamlet. You go back and go to bed. You've got to get up early in the morning."

When he heard this he stood still watching her walk away. She took a few steps away before coming back to him. "I forgot to congratulate you," she said with a smile. "We must shake hands."

She took his powerful hand and shook it, then said once more, "You go back and go to bed." Only then did she hurry off.

He was beside himself with happiness, feeling much lighter as he thought of going to the wood after his meal the next day. He did not wait for her but went straight home. He saw a figure flit past near by. It was too dark for him to see exactly who it was so he paid no attention to it but went to bed the moment he got in as she had told him.

She did not come back that night.

With the passage of time Little Sister stopped crying for the woman who had loved and taught her. She seemed a lot older now and wanted to do many things that she could and should do. The family was peaceful again now and life was back on course. But it was a new course. They no longer suffered from useless panic. They did not mourn or become worked up with indignation. Facts forced them to a deeper understanding. They could see further now so that they no longer sought peace in a retreat from the world, but worked even harder than ever. Now the whole family held meetings to discuss everything, often bringing other people in too. When the meetings broke up Zhao Desheng would echo his sons' views and say, "Right, we'll see. Let's decide after the harvest."

The family was more full of bustle and life than before. The land in this beautiful hamlet belonged to others, but they believed this would not go on for ever. A new order was soon going to appear, a new order that they would create themselves.

1933

A Certain Night

A muffled tramp of feet.

A group of figures, too many to be counted, came into the square from the hall that was lit with bluish electric lights. The heavy tramp of boots and shoes in the thick snow. The ferocious wind of a winter's night lashing their faces with the rain that had been falling for a fortnight and with large snowflakes. The sudden onslaught of the cold wind made them all shiver in their hearts, but they tramped on.

Another howling blast of wind mercilessly flailed their bodies and faces. In the middle of them all, surrounded and driven along by a huge escort, came one man, a slight young man looking handsome and at the same time drawn. The shock seemed to wake him up. Everything that had happened in the past or just a moment ago seemed set out before him, at a great distance and very clearly. That cunning face, malicious and smug, a round face, a face with a revolting moustache of the sort imperialists wear; and an evil voice giving a forced laugh. From where he sat up on high he had given him such an arrogant and uninhibited stare. "Have you anything else to say?" he had asked, then continued, "You have been given your sentences and they will be executed immediately." When the young man remembered this a fire that could have consumed him started up in his heart. He had wanted to rip that face to shreds and smash the voice to smithereens. In his wild fury he almost longed to push his way out through the men crowding round him and start walking fast and vigorously. Just now, when he had been suddenly condemned to death without any trial, he had not stayed calm like the rest of his comrades, but had passed out, overwhelmed by extreme anger and pain.

He was a passionate poet, loyal and hard-working.

A rifle butt thudded hard into his chest, which was even more emaciated than usual after twenty days of being kept on short rations and going hungry in the dark and sunless prison.

"What are you in such a hurry for, f --- you? Death's waiting for you. You'll get yours." A murderous-looking soldier started swearing at him after breaking the silence by hitting him.

The manacles and fetters on his hands and feet clanked repulsively, as did those on other hands and feet. Then there was even more noise around him as iron-soled boots tramped harder in the snow.

He now understood some more, and realized where he was now being taken. A strange thought came into his head. Above his eyes he could see another pair of eyes, a pair of beloved and unforgettable eyes that could always see his soul. He was very clearly aware of something deep in his heart that was pricking him then agonizingly tearing his flesh and blood inch by inch.

The sky was black, boundlessly black, and from it fell rain and snow while the north wind howled. The world was grey, like fog, and the deathly grey was reflected in the night by the snow. The people were black figures moving silently across the snow. Amid the sound of shackles and bayonets none of the escorts or prisoners spoke, groaned, sighed or wept. They moved without interruption to the square that had been secretly turned into a temporary execution ground.

"F --- them, the swine," thought some of them. "Where are they taking us to bump us off?"

A woman comrade in the second rank kept shaking her thick mop of hair as if she were angry. It was because the wind kept blowing her short hair across her forehead and eyes.

The young man forced himself by biting his lips hard not to give a wild and rending final shout. He was shaking with a fury that he could not express and glaring all around with a look of hatred so fierce that it hurt him, looking for something as if he wished he could devour it all, looking at one person and then at another.

The dim light of the snow shone on the man next to him, a fierce-browed soldier, and on another stupid soldier with his mouth and nostrils open wide, and on. . . . Suddenly he saw a familiar and friendly face, which showed him a calm, kindly expression, an expression that spoke volumes, an expression of consolation and encouragement that only comrades can give each other as they face their death. Most of his hatred and regrets disappeared. Affection and something else that can only be called life filled his wounded chest. All he wanted to do was to hug that face and kiss it. He replied to the expression with a much braver and a resolute nod.

The tramp of feet, a loud and untidy noise in the darkness, was like the irregular pounding of victory drums crowded all around them, the twenty-five of them, as they walked ahead. Above their heads the wind was roaring and soughing, as if a great red banner were waving above them.

"Halt! This is the place. Where d'you think you're going, you f --- ers?" The chief executioner was armed and struck his Mauser pistol hard as he shouted in a firm voice with all his intimidating might.

"We're there," was the thought that echoed in many minds.

"Line the criminals up! Tie them up." The loathsome and vicious order came from the chief executioner's throat, and the soldiers in their padded greatcoats pushed them clumsily and hard, hitting them with rifle butts and putting ropes round their chests to tie them to the stakes behind them. There was an even louder noise of leather boots and shoes in the snow.

They said not a word, holding hard to their anger and their silence because they could no longer find any way of expressing their hatred for these enemies. Their hands and feet were now shackled and they were each tied fast to a wooden post that had been driven in days earlier.

Darkness stretched out in front of them, wind, rain and snow kept blowing into their faces, and the bone-chilling cold was mercilessly lashing their bodies, from which the warm scholars' gowns and overcoats had been ripped off in the hall. But they did not feel cold.

They were standing in a close-packed row.

"Here, over here a bit. Aim straight. . . ."

In the darkness of the night a group of men could just be made out in front of them carrying and moving around something heavy.

"Right. Here will do. Count the criminals."

"One, two, three. . . ." A soldier walked up to them and started counting.

The chief executioner, his face set in an ugly cast, followed the soldier along the row of prisoners, bending his fingers as he counted.

At the sight of that ugly and vicious face, which seemed to symbolize the cruelty of all the rulers to the oppressed, an angry fire started to burn in his heart again. The fire hurt his eyes and his whole body. He longed to be able to punch and kill the cur, but he had been tied up tightly with his hands behind him. All he could do was to grind his teeth in hatred, his whole body shaking with fury.

"Courage, comrade," said a comrade standing to his right.

He turned and saw that it was a familiar face: the man with whom he ɪ ˙ ˙ talked a great deal at supper.

"It's not that. I'm rather worked up."

". . . twenty-three, twenty-four, twenty-five. Correct. Right. . . ."

The men who were counting started yelling and stamping hard in the snow as they moved towards the object that had been set up.

Boundless emptiness, wind, snow, grey, darkness. . . . Human forms looked big and heavy against the deathly pale grey.

"Very well. Ready. Wait for my order."

So shouted the chief executioner.

All hearts tensed, pulled tight like bowstrings. The heavy death-like thing stood in front of them, carefully guarded by several soldiers. The sky was about to fall and the darkness to crush them, the twenty-five.

Someone started shouting in a loud voice:

"Arise, comrades.   Don't forget that although we're going to die now a great congress is being held elsewhere today, and our government is going to be formed today. We must celebrate the creation of our government. Long live our government!"

With that they all broke out into wild shouts. There had been many things in their minds that they had forgotten to say or express.   Only now did they suddenly realize, which was why they were all shouting at the tops of their voices the slogans they wanted to shout, dispelling the darkness. What spread out in front of them was the brilliance of a new state being founded.

As a whistle blew shrilly a mighty sound rose from twenty-five voices starting to sing:

"Arise, ye prisoners of starvation. . . ."

There was a rattle of fire as the heavy object raked along the whole length of the row, firing several dozen rounds.

The singing was quieter, but some voices were now even louder:

"It is the final struggle. . . ."

The whistle blew again.

Another rattle of fire as the row was raked for a second time with several dozen more rounds.

The more bullets that were fired, the quieter was the singing. There were now only a few voices still shouting.

"The Interna. . . ."

The whistle blew for the third time and the third burst of firing began.   With the sound of the bullets the singing stopped.

"Try singing now, you c -- ts, you bastards."

The chief executioner swore at them with an air of

satisfaction, then walked back the way they had come, giving his orders:

"Put the gun away, and get back to barracks as soon as you can. The bodies can be buried tomorrow morning. The dead can't run away."

With that he walked back towards the hall.

Several dozen soldiers once again tramped noisily through the snow as they returned.

The night was silent, hushed, solemn. Large snow-flakes and fine drops of rain were swirling around. The wild, winter wind blew first one way then another. Snow piled up on the head that hung forward, only to be dispersed by the wind. None of them said anything, tied there in silence. In a few places, in one, two, three ... places, blood was flowing and falling on the snow in the darkness.

When will it be light?

1933

Rushing

THE brown of the unnamed hills that separated him from his home was beginning to emerge from the darkness. They were forming a soft, clear line against the translucent, red-tinged sky. Another gust of cold dawn wind blew across the red brick buildings from the desolate fields and on into the trees opposite. During the night the wind had roared like a tiger, but though it was now no louder than the hooting of an owl it still chilled the bone. When Thick Zhang could hear the wind was far away he pushed with his back against Wang the Second, who was leaning against him as they both squatted there, and mumbled, as if to himself.

"Dawn." His red, suppurating eyes moved a crack away from the sleeves into which his hands were tucked to gaze gloomily in the direction of his home.

He stretched out his two big feet with their rough straw sandals over a pair of worn-out padded shoes. His feet had been tucked under his thighs. He shook his legs and stood up. Standing bent-backed, he took a step forward, stopped and said:

"Ought to be here any time now. At dawn, they said...." He said no more but crouched, sat down again, and shivered once more.

More big feet in straw sandals were stretched out by Zhang's legs. Another man stood up and walked over to the corner of the wall to take a noisy piss. By now it was dawn, and the sky was aglow with colour. At the other end of the red building a scrawny, pathetic cockerel shook its wings, stretched its neck and started to crow. The man who had been pissing did not squat down again when he came back, but leaned against the wall to rub the sleep out of his eyes. A feeble yellow glow still came from the electric light that was hanging in front of him. A few countrymen hurried in from somewhere: from the big bundles they were carrying they looked like small traders. These newcomers looked at them then stood apart, talking about something together. They knew that the train would soon arrive. Two more men stood up to stretch limbs that were numb after being bent for so long.

The scrawny, pathetic lad in uniform, who had been seen rushing around busily every time a train came and went during the night, emerged again, coughing. He walked round in a circle, glancing at the clock on the wall, then cast a look of mingled pity and contempt at the crowd of yokels who had endured most of the night in the cold wind there. "This way," he finally said.

Just then the clock chimed imposingly. It was the third time they had heard it.

They stood up and followed the man in uniform, their swollen bodies bent, to the little doorway where tickets were sold. The man said something then went away. They looked at the doorway, not hearing what he said.

"Sixty cents in silver, fourth class. One at a time now." Inside the doorway the lamplight fell on a little counter where the ticket seller in a cotton-padded gown was shrugging his shoulders as he spoke irritably, his eyes with too little sleep. Everyone who bought a ticket cast an envious glance at the little teapot with a broken spout that was apparently steaming beside him.

A snowy white silver dollar landed on the counter with a ring that cut straight to the heart. Without a word being spoken the forty cents' worth of banknotes given as change were tucked inside the man's clothes. There was no need to count them. It was only forty cents. Then he stepped aside.

"What the hell! We'll be there in a few hours." Thick Zhang watched as Qiao the Third anxiously felt the pouch in which he carried his money then made this remark to comfort him. He found himself a little comforted by it too.

"Hmh." Qiao the Third went with him to the platform, where there were several other people he had not seen before, including one in a long gown who was probably a student.

Fiery red was now coming from the sun. Thick steam rose between the branches of the sparse and distant trees, from behind which came a great screech of wheels. With two toots of its whistle the train drew in to the little platform, step by step, panting and sweating, and dragging its steam.

There was a rush towards a door on the train, and everyone else crowded after. Some people were pushed out of the train to block the little doorway, and other people started quarrelling. Then a loud voice shouted, "Where do you think you're going? This is third class!" At this the crowd bunched anxiously together, stared stupidly, rushed towards another doorway, and all finally squeezed into a carriage.

The dirty old carriage was crammed full of piles of disorderly cotton cloth on which was an untidy row of heads that were at an angle or hanging forward. On some the mouths were wide open, revealing yellow teeth and emitting a powerful stench, while snores came from the gaping nostrils. Some heads, long unshaven and with matted hair, lolled forward, strings of dribble hanging from their open mouths to the chests below. Some people had their eyes open as they gazed out of the train or at the crowd now entering. They neither moved nor spoke.

"Zhang, brother, there's a place here."

"Go over there. They can squeeze another one in."

The people who had been woken up shifted themselves along then went back to sleep. Others rubbed their eyes and gazed at the closed windows, now misted over.

The train had been going at full speed for some time.

"Hey, this train, or whatever it's called, is quite something. Look at those hills and trees, turning around like ghosts, turning and vanishing."

Wang the Second twisted his head round to rest it against the glass. Long's sleeve had already wiped the mist off a part of the window. They were all excited by the warmth in the carriage and the amazing scenes outside it. The sun's slanting beams painted many yellow bands of light inside the carriage. Many people were sitting up straight because of the yellow light.

Qiao the Third patted his pouch again, thinking of his family's property. Everything he had in his bag made him feel rather uneasy. The only reason why he was going to Shanghai with this crowd of people was because his wife had driven him to do it. He wasn't at all sure he was doing the right thing. He repeated once again what he had said many times already:

"Brother Zhang! Don't ditch me when you get to Shanghai. I haven't got friends or relations there like the rest of you. Whatever happens, you've got to find me somewhere to stay. I've only got a bit of money with me. . . ."

"Have I got more than you? All I've got is what I staked my life to borrow: one silver dollar and four ten-cent notes. We'll sort everything out when we get to Shanghai. Don't be so cowardly." Li Xianglin pushed his lipless mouth into the conversation to say this.

"Yes, we'll be fine when we find them. Shanghai's a big place, not like where we come from. Lots of people with plenty of money. It'll be easy making a living there." Zhang's suppurating eyelids glanced in the direction of home a number of times. He thought of the breakfast rice porridge that must be cooking about now, then of the peck of rice they had borrowed and the two baskets of chaff left over. No need to worry about food. "As long as I can find a job," he continued, "I'll have nothing to fear from Scabby Sun. Dammit. When we settle up with him in the summer he'll get three hundredweight from each of us at once. If grain's a bit cheaper then there should be enough for a third of an acre."

"If we can pay it back it doesn't matter if we have to pay even more. All I'm worried about is. . . ." Qiao the Third bowed his head as he spoke.

Old Long pulled a dry steamed breadroll out of his pocket while the others gnawed at the coarse grain griddle cakes they had brought with them from home. Their conversation grew more animated.

"It was worth it after all. Spending most of the night in that northwest wind was nothing much, but sixty cents in silver is several days' food. You can stand cold, but you can't go without food."

"There's no difference between third and fourth class. If there was a fifth class we'd have gone fifth class and have saved twice as much."

"How many hours to get to Shanghai? Five? It's expensive. Sixty cents in silver for five hours! That's two thousand copper cash."

Their fellow travellers sitting beside them, though strangers, joined in their conversation. Some of them had been to Shanghai but did not know much about the situation there. They talked to each other about the hardships at home and why they were travelling. There was not much difference between them. When the talk moved on to the harvest and the state of the market the atmosphere in the carriage gradually livened up even more. Some women sat down at the other end opened up the front of their jackets, and stuffed the great pendulous bags of their breasts into the mouths of their crying babies. By now the sun was casting a sheet of sunlight in through every window. The jolting of the train made it dance on every dried out face and filthy cotton garment. The people in the carriage who had squatted by a wall in the cold wind for most of the night began to doze off because of the warmth and the coarse flour in their stomachs. Their eyelids gradually shut and the talk fell off as fresh snoring came from beside some other people who had now woken up.

The train whistle shrieked over and over again as the black smoke and white steam swept along the train and the engine's wheels turned with desperate speed. The passengers all became animated. "Look! Foreign build-

ings! Look at those chimneys. They're factories." The
train had reached Shanghai.

The long train drew into the station, stopping at
Platform 6. Through dozens of doors the train disgorged
its crowd of people from so many villages and country
towns. The six bumpkins kept close together as they
rushed towards the exit with everyone else. Porters were
crowded in among ladies with powdered faces and fur
coats, ladies who hung on gentlemen's arms while the
gentlemen, their heads held high, hurried past the
bumpkins in the rush for the exit. It might have been
a race. The adults shouted, the children joined in too.
Some of the people who had run ahead came hurrying
back again. "Damn it, good gracious," someone was
saying.

The anxious and the timid rushed from one group to
another, crowding together till they reached the street.

"Pigs!" A driver stretched his head out to swear at
them. The black car brushed past, almost crushing
them under a wheel.

At the sight of the rickshaws rushing towards them
they turned back to make way. A woman in a cheongsam
was just behind them. "Damn you!" she said in a
biting voice through her blood-red lips.

The bumpkins stood on a street corner discussing
what to do. After their conference they pressed on again,
having chosen Thick Zhang to take the lead and ask
the way. Zhang stared hard with his suppurating eyes.
He turned his smiling face till he saw people who looked quite kindly, then went up to them and asked, "Could
you tell me the way to Wujia Corner?"

Some answered with a shake of the head, and some
said, "West, I think. Ask again later."

"Look at that lot: real hicks," was what all the young women whispered as they pointed at them in passing.

"Hey, look at that doll: stark naked. Looks quite real. If I had the money I'd take a little one back home and stand her on the cupboard in the kitchen. That would be great." Never in their lives had they seen some of the splendid things in the department stores, which they kept going to look at. Then when they had been gazing for some time they seemed to remember something and said, "Let's move. We'd better find the place first."

"Hey, Qiao the Third, Shanghai women look funny. Dressed like foreign devils, aren't they?" said someone, as if he had forgotten his worries.

After walking along first one street then another they had left the busier part of the city for a district with cobbled roads and only low cramped buildings beside them. Beside the road were little stalls surrounded by dirty children wiping the snot from their noses with their hands and gazing at the peanuts on the stalls. There were even more appallingly badly behaved children wearing tattered hats and rolling about mischievously in the middle of the road. Handcarts loaded with stones, cinders or dung squeaked and rumbled along as they carefully avoided the children, who were like a herd of wild horses. When an occasional lorry came past, the children first shouted then ran behind it for a while before running back. Hairless and apparently homeless old dogs lay there helplessly, their bellies shrivelled, gazing with their strange eyes at the passers-by.

When they asked the way again and found out that they were almost there their spirits began to rise once more. They felt things were looking rather more hopeful for them.   As this hope drew a little closer the sun was shining on them from high above.   Zhang, who was walking in front, spoke again:

"I haven't seen him for three years, but my brother-in-law's a real tough guy.   He could do enough field work for two, but his luck was out and he ran into some soldiers who took him off with them.   He had to work as a porter for them for six months.   By the time he escaped and got back home his landlord had let his land to someone else. Anyhow, there's not much money to be made on the land, so when he couldn't get the land back he left in a fury and brought his old woman to Shanghai with him.   He found a way out of his troubles. They say he's earning a good dozen dollars a month. I'd be very satisfied if I had a job like that. If I go to his place now he might be out, but my sister's bound to be in."

"Zhang, old brother, don't ditch us when you land on your feet.   People depend on their parents at home and on their friends when they're away. We're all counting on you. . . ."   Qiao the Third spoke anxiously.

"Never," said Zhang vehemently. "We came here together and we'll share whatever we can get. If I start work before you I'll lend you some money, don't worry."

"If your brother-in-law's out we'll go to see Uncle Zhao the Fourth.   Where does your uncle live, Long?"

"I'm not sure, but I do know he works in the Japanese cotton mill. If we ask at the factory we'll find out sooner or later." Only then did Long remember that a few years back he had fought with Uncle Zhao the Fourth over a basket of sweet potatoes and hurt Zhao's head badly.   He might not be able to count on Zhao's help in getting him a job now he'd come to Shanghai.   He felt a secret twinge of regret and tried to cheer himself up by telling himself, "An uncle's an uncle when all's said and done. He won't let me starve to death."

They asked their way again and turned into a lane, at the end of which were several compounds in which stood a jumble of little tiled houses and thatched huts. Even in the winter sun the rubbish in the yards stank.

Stepping over a puddle, Zhang stood by a gate in a bamboo fence and shouted at the top of his voice, "Li Yongfa! Li Yongfa!"

The face of a girl of twelve or thirteen emerged from beside the nappies drying on a bamboo pole. Her eyes were wide with astonishment as she stared at him, and her thin brownish hair made her look even uglier. A head with untidy hair was thrust out of a side room. Goodness only knew what it was that hung outside the window. On either side of the house were piles of broken glass bottles and pottery jars as well as rags. There seemed to be footsteps inside the house, but nobody paid them any attention.

"Li Yongfa! Li Yongfa! Sister!"

"Hey, Fa, looks like someone wants you." The voice came from the unkempt head.

Li Yongfa came out of the room to the east. He was stripped to the waist and holding a short padded jacket. His strong, reddish peasant's chest had now fallen in, and his sunken face was so changed that Zhang could not recognize him. He recognized Zhang, however, and came over to him without waiting to put his jacket on, waving a shrivelled arm, shaking and calling out:

"Thicky! Welcome!"

But his laugh dried up the moment he saw the crowd behind Zhang, and he said no more. Zhang went on talking. He had expected to be smiling but he did not smile. His changed brother-in-law was not only a pathetic stranger, he had also given him what amounted to a terrible shock. He could not laugh, but only said, "I didn't recognize you. You've aged. Have you been ill? How's my sister?"

"Come in. Did you all come together? That's Wang the Second. I recognized you. Yes, I have changed. When all's said and done, working on the land's best. Come inside." He put on his padded jacket and led them inside.

The front room was packed full of things such as beds and a coal stove. There was just a narrow way through to the little back room that Li Yongfa rented for two dollars a month. When they all trooped in they filled it to overflowing. As their eyes were used to the sunlight this room seemed even darker than it was. Li Yongfa dragged out a bench and urged them to sit on it as he asked, "Have you just arrived in Shanghai?"

"Is that you, Thicky?" a woman curled up on the bed in a heap of cotton wadding asked with a groan.

As Zhang went over to the bed none of the others spoke. There were things, things they had never known before, weighing on their hearts.

"Thicky, you've come at just the right time. Your sister thinks of you all every day. She misses you terribly. She says she wishes she could see a single tree in here. If I could get the money together I'd have taken her home long ago. I hear you had a good harvest last year. Would I be able to get an acre or so of land to work if we went back, I wonder."

"Mm...."

"You can see I've got a lot thinner. I haven't been

ill, but I just can't take working fourteen hours a day. The machines squeeze all the life out of you. I suppose I'm lucky I haven't been crushed to death by one. But I'm not going to survive. . . . What have you come here for, Thicky?"

"Thicky, how's everything at home? At least you get something to eat there. I've miscarried again. There was a strike in the factory the other day and I fell over." The woman's terrible face emerged from the tattered cotton wadding. She looked like an old witch.

"Oh, it's not so bad. . . ."

"We want to go back, Thicky. Will you help us by asking around for some way I can make a living? There really are no jobs to be found in Shanghai. It's impossible for us here. I've been out of work for over two months and she's bedbound. Thicky! What are you all doing here?"

Zhang could find no reply. He bit his lips, looking in anger at the faces of the people he could not believe were his relations. He could find no words of comfort for this couple on the verge of starving to death. He was furious with them, blaming them for everything he found disgusting. He felt they had tricked him, had tricked them all, into coming to Shanghai by telling them how easy it was to find work and earn money. He was angry with them for being out of work and only wished he could hit them or the men who had come with him. But that crowd were all glaring at him like wild animals holding their fury in check. They looked as though they wanted to hit him. Unable to control himself among these ferocious glares, Qiao the Third started sobbing.

Evening came, and the murky sun was sinking ponderously behind some houses as the crowd of men were still rushing along the streets. Rushing along with them were people going home from work. They looked with envy at the workers, whose heads hung low as they dragged their weary feet along, gazing blankly ahead with fixed, grey, stupefied and exhausted stares. They could not think about what was beside them. Squeezed among them as they too rushed along were some sallow-faced women who looked barely human, their hair and clothing still covered with cotton wool from the mill, cotton wool that flew from their heads all over the place. The men stared and stared, and started feeling sorry for the people they saw. But this feeble pity was no match for the terror they felt on their own account. They became more short-tempered than ever. Wang the Second glared at Old Long in fury and said abusively:

"All you know is that it's a Japanese mill. Do you know how many Japanese mills there are in Shanghai?"

"No. Do you? All he's ever called it is the Japanese mill."

"Stop quarrelling, stop quarrelling. We'd better find somewhere where we can get a drink of water and eat something. Tomorrow you can all come over to Pudong with me. I had a letter from my uncle a few days ago. He's bound to have jobs for us, so there's no need to quarrel," interjected Li Xianglin.

"Fine, fine." As Zhang went into a little teahouse with them he remembered his sister lying on the bed after her miscarriage. All she had to eat was a little millet gruel. She was longing for someone to buy her a griddle cake with a bit of lard dripping inside, but this was more than her husband could provide. "I'll buy her some," he thought. "I've still got a dollar and forty cents. . . ."

They sat in a corner of the teahouse and asked for a pot of tea as each of them brought some left-over dry bread out of his bundle to gnaw. This only left their empty stomachs feeling emptier than ever: a little flour could not satisfy a craving even fiercer than hunger. Wang the Second spoke irritably again:

"Do you know exactly where your uncle lives?"

"In Jiajiachang in Pudong, not far from the British-American Tobacco Factory. He's been working there for five years. He'll probably be able to. . . ."

"He may have a job, but he won't be able to keep all of us. And even if he can find you a job he won't necessarily be able to find anything for us. Didn't you see his brother-in-law? It's the same with him. He's supporting two families back there." Qiao the Third put his remark in.

"Damned Japanese mill, Japanese mill. . . ." Old Long clenched his fist tighter than ever as the hatred for Zhao the Fourth that had faded away came rushing back into his heart. He wished he could get hold of him and thump him.

The people on the next table were talking very animatedly. There was one lad wearing a torn lined jacket. He had a grey face and grey hair, and from his build could not have been more than sixteen, but his face looked old. He took a deep pull on the cigarette in his left hand while waving his right hand in circles as he continued:

"Once I heard the whistle my heart was in my mouth. I realized things were bad. Then there was a rattle of gunfire, and you know how many people were killed.

There were dozens of workers lying on the ground, and four or five of them at least never came round. It was that Wang who gave the order to fire, damn him: he's the deputy manager. Killing a few workers is nothing to them. If you want to make trouble he'll bloody well lock you out. Then where will several thousands of you find your next meal? There's a strike now, demanding the killer's life, compensation payments and medical expenses. If you ask me, it's pointless. This isn't the first time workers have been killed. Goodness only knows how many strikes there've been, and they always go back to work because their stomachs can't take it. What I say is just kill them. Don't tell me we couldn't run the factory ourselves."

"Who are you going to kill?" asked another who was a little older but had the same grey face and hair. "You want to act, but before you can touch a hair on their heads you'll find yourself already in trouble. Everything takes time. Some people still believe that their bosses are good. Some would rather starve than take action. Others have sold out to the capitalists to slaughter workers. Everything has to be done properly. Sitting here shouting is useless, and killing a few managers would be useless too. What we have to do now is to make all the workers understand and unite for the fight. That's why we have to lay down conditions and stop them from firing workers. Don't be impatient, my lad. One day. . . ."

As they listened to this they were speechless with astonishment. Then someone else who was sitting at the table in front of them stopped a young beggar who had just made his way in and asked:

"How's your father's arm, Jin? Has your mum found

herself a fancy man yet? Your father had better accept the way things are. If he's not prepared to let his
wife have other men he won't eat. He should get a bit
of money together while his missus is still young. What
have you come barging in here for, you little bastard?
If you don't look out people will take you for a pick-
pocket and throw you into jail to feed the lice."

"Fuck your mother, and fuck your gran too," cursed
the young beggar as he ran outside.

"Damned little pig," the man said, turning to look at
them. "You wouldn't know about it. His old man's
in the same shop as me. Last month his eyes went all
of a blur — I don't know why — he shouted, and collapsed unconscious. One arm was trapped in the belt
and all bloody. A lot of the flesh was torn off, and
then it flew down to hit him on the head. We all
thought he was done for, but he didn't die. He lies in
his bed all day, groaning. He'll never work again in
his life. The factory gave him ten dollars and that was
that. His wife had nothing to eat, so she had to find
herself fancy men. Their boy spends his days begging
and stealing. You probably don't yet realize how tough
it is being a worker in Shanghai. You're new here.
There are lots of places in Shanghai where you can go
and enjoy yourself. You can watch operas for hours
and hours on a twenty-cent ticket. The French concession's worth a look at too. There's a fourteen-storey
building, and the cars parked outside it look like ants.
Hey, what's your trade?"

A lot of people were staring at them, and they all
looked at each other, not knowing what to say. It was
Zhang once more who found the courage to reply,

"We're looking for relations. We've come to Shanghai to find work."

At this some people burst out into rude laughter, the sound of which made them shudder. Someone said angrily, "I suppose enough people haven't starved to death in Shanghai for you. Is that why you had to come here to die? There are hundreds of thousands of people out of work here."

"There's nothing to eat in the countryside either. What we harvested all went to the landlord. We even had to repay him for the dung. We didn't have a single grain left in the house. I had to borrow two dollars for the journey. For that two dollars, the price of a peck of rice, I'll have to give him three bushels of rice in the summer. I didn't know what it was like here in Shanghai. If I had I wouldn't have come."

"If you've got no rice, demand some from your landlord, like we do when we demand work from the capitalists. You let your sweat and blood fall drop by drop on the land, and they squeeze our flesh and blood bit by bit in the workshop. . . ."

A lot of people surrounded them in the teahouse, and they became the centre of the conversation. Everyone put in their word, but nothing that was said could bring them even a moment's peace of mind. It only made them find it all even more unbearable. Unable to sit there any longer, they left the teahouse. "What am I to do?" grumbled old Qiao the Third. "I'd better take the train back."

"We'll go to Pudong first thing tomorrow. Let's talk everything over after we've found my uncle. Things might be better there." So Li Xianglin was thinking to himself.

"Where can I buy some griddle cakes with lard?" Thick Zhang blinked his red, suppurating eyelids again.

The moon rose in the direction of home; at least, that was where home ought to be. The countryside was still, apart from one or two barks from distant dogs. The stars flashed their gloomy eyes above their heads, the moon occasionally hid behind the thin, scudding clouds, and the wind was the same cold, gusty wind. The birds sleeping on the branches turned uneasily as the waters of the stream gurgled and the railway lines stretched out, apparently without end, across stream after stream, skirting one low ridge after another. Walking along the railway were two men, one tall and one short, heading for home.

The taller one in front gazed at the distant horizon that disappeared into the darkness, blinked his suppurating eyes, lifted his hand to wipe away his tears and said:

"If I'd known before I'd have gone with old Qiao the Third. It'd have been better to have had a place on a train. How much further do you think there is to go?"

Wang the Second, who was following a step behind, looked up into the distance and said, "Don't ask. Just keep going. When we get to a place where there's a hut we can shelter from the wind and spend the night. We'll carry on walking tomorrow and the day after. We'll see then."

"Oh. . . ."

The two of them walked along in silence, neither of them wanting to speak. Thick Zhang saw his sister's face again, that terrifying dead face. He remembered her ghostly body again, dressed only in a thin jacket . . . not that he could blame his brother-in-law. His memories then turned to other things, to the beggars and the women weeping over the bodies of their husbands who had been shot when the factory manager opened fire. Then he thought of the little room he had gone to with his brother-in-law where people were shooting morphine. The addicts had all been monstrously thin and dark and covered with needle pricks: his brother-in-law had told him that without their shots they could not make themselves work, but that their shots would kill them sooner or later. Then he thought of. . . . He remembered so many things, and felt that the sky was gradually crushing him. His breathing came fast, and he simply could not look at anything else.

"Wang the Second!" he shouted. "Wang the Second!"

Wang the Second suddenly hurried forward to grab him and shouted, "Thicky! Thicky!"

The two of them stood there for a moment with their arms around each other before pulling themselves together and walking on side by side.

"I feel really sorry about it."

"Forget it, forget it. Li Xianglin's a bad lot too. I'm sure he's found his uncle and forgotten about us."

"Not necessarily. Maybe he's even worse off than us. Young Liu's with him. Liu's a good bloke anyway."

"What Long said was right, Thicky. He said that the Shanghai workers have a future. Because they stand together he's going to stay with them. But we can stand together too. If young Long stays in Shanghai, that'll only be one beggar the more."

"Hey, Second, do you know any way of paying back those three bushels of rice?"

With that they both fell silent again as they bent their

heads to let the fierce wind blow across them. There was not a sound as their feet tramped along.

From far away wheels could be heard. Then the train's headlight came into sight as its black smoke stained the pitch black sky, and then the train flew towards them, rushed past and rolled on. It was a Shanghai train, and in the lighted fourth-class carriages were more groups of country folk fleeing to Shanghai because they could not get by in the country. They were asleep in there, their mouths gaping and dribbling as they dreamed their pathetic and absurd dreams.

After this violent noise had passed by the countryside was still once more. Wang the Second answered with ferocity from the twisted corner of his mouth, "Three bushels of rice? We know how to do it. Just wait, Scabby Sun!"

1933

The Reunion

IT was the beginning of the third year since they had moved to the countryside. Although spring had been a little late, the Clear and Bright Festival was almost upon them. The willow branches planted the previous year had been in leaf for some time, and their sparse fronds were hanging over the pond. A few little blossoming peach trees among them added touches of pink. The little hills, near and far, were grey-green with the old pines that covered them, but they too had some attractive fresh greens on them; and the wild azaleas that grew among the new grass and on the mossy crags were dense with blossom. Larks and many other strange birds with long white tails sang loudly, and at dawn tiny orioles started their clear and mellifluous calls as they flew between the trees. Some insects scurried around while other, brightly-coloured, winged ones danced and flew through the spring scenery. All that had previously been still was now moving; all that had been dead had now revived. The breath of life was everywhere.

But indoors, in the house that still felt old and stale despite having been renovated, the fire was still glowing in the room with a sunken hearth. The fuel was the roots of old pines that had been sawn down during the winter. Because they had not dried right out, and also for the sake of frugality, a thick layer of rice husks had been spread over the wood, damping down the fire and sending up thick smoke that coiled around the rafters before slowly and gently making its way out through the lattice in the door. Wherever the smoke usually lingered there hung black tassel-like objects of varied lengths and thicknesses which made the room even darker. All around the hearth stood a number of round-backed willow armchairs of different sizes on which the family would gather when they were not busy. In winter, and especially when there was hot tea and some taros to roast in the ashes, there really was a warm family atmosphere. But now, in the spring sunlight that was already beginning to warm up, all the chairs were empty except for the biggest one with its square arms, in which old Mr Lu was squatting, wrapped in a tattered wolf-skin rug. He was alone. As a former official and an educated man he disliked grumbling, so he sometimes read a novel, but whenever he heard footsteps nearby he would lift his head to listen, longing for someone to come in and talk to him. If the passer-by was his youngest daughter Purity he would twist his beard and shout, "Hey, come and fill my pipe."

The pipe, with its stem over a foot long, would go into his mouth. The pipe had been his for very many years, sharing weal and woe with him for half a life-time. The pristine freshness of its jade mouthpiece and ivory bowl had long ago given way to dirty yellow. Since moving to the country he had only smoked home-grown tobacco.

"This tobacco smells horrible, Dad," Purity often said as she filled the pipe. Another of her remarks was, "This tobacco's awful. I just can't understand you, Dad." She disliked this chore, although every time he saw her, her brown face bubbling with innocence and life, he felt a kind of lightness and his empty old heart felt another kind of satisfaction. He always answered her in a kindly voice.

"Mm. It's fine. Comes from our own garden, and as your mother knows how to cure the leaves they're absolutely pure. You're too young to understand. It's marvellous tobacco."

Old Mr Lu was a man of nearly sixty. Only a few years earlier he had still been a powerful man. He used to work for a company in a good job, but first there had been September 18th, and after that January 28th.* Although he had not bothered himself much with such matters, the company had been affected and had closed down. A lot of his friends and relations had lost their jobs at about the same time, so that after rushing around looking for other work for a while he had ended up having to come back home in the hope of eking out his days on a bit of land that had long been in his family. As he had grown used to doing things in style when younger he found it very depressing to spend his declining years in this run-down way. He had aged fast, especially after a serious illness early in the autumn of the previous year from which he had not yet fully recovered.

Although the illness was nothing serious or alarming it had dragged on for a good six months. He had not been very clear in the head, often talking in his sleep. His hands and feet had felt numb and dead because of a nervous disorder. He had always been mumbling on,

---

* On 18 September 1931 Japan started the military action that resulted in her seizure of the northeastern provinces; and on 28 January 1932 Japanese forces launched an all-out attack on Shanghai.

asking for news about his son who had disappeared after losing his job and worrying about the future of his other son who had come home after having to break off his schooling. Later on that son had found a minor government appointment in a neighbouring province, for which he had set out with a little bedroll and vast ambitions. The son who had disappeared had also turned up again, staying in a cousin's house and waiting for his luck to change. The young often have all sorts of wild and exaggerated ideas that their elders cannot understand. From then on the old man had begun to pull round, but although he seemed to have recovered some time ago he was still very sensitive to cold and spent a lot of time alone by the fire that everyone else wanted to avoid. Things had never been like that before, as he himself often realized.

"The sun's nice and warm today, Dad, so why don't we take the chair out for you to sit outside?" His second wife, who was twenty years his junior and still had the high spirits of a youngster, asked him this question once or twice every day. She now spent all her days with her sleeves rolled high, busy in the kitchen, washing clothes in the pond, or supervising her youngest boy as he fed the pigs. Although she had driven away the only girl who might have been of any help to her earlier that year she did not find the life hard. That her youngest boy and the fourth son had dropped out of school made the place livelier as far as she was concerned.

"It's windy ... there's some wind. ... I don't like wind. ... I'll go out tomorrow." Such were the old man's hesitant replies as he put it off each day. He did rather want to see the sunshine, but he felt that